MASSACRE!

△△△△△△△△△△△△

Into the wood he pl
now. Those lance sha
scarlet and black fe
nunni.

The sun was below the horizon when he came into
a larger clearing, where the skin houses his tribe
used in summer, while moving after the game,
were set haphazardly along the meandering stream
cutting through the center of the rough circle.

The houses were collapsing, burning. Bodies lay
on the ground . . .

△△△△△△△△△△△△△

"Ardath Mayhar takes a bold look at the mysterious
Anasazi . . . with the patience of a skilled archaeol-
ogist, she has picked away the centuries to reveal . . . *people*. Her characters are living, breathing men and women who laugh, cry, love and
marry, share jokes and sadness. Equally well de-
scribed is their homeland, harsh yet beautiful, demanding but rewarding.

"May we see more of Ardath Mayhar's Anasazi,
the Ancient Ones of the Mesa."

—Don Coldsmith,
author of *The Spanish Bit Saga*
and *The Changing Wind*

"Ardath Mayhar's work is swift and sure and enter-
taining. A real treat for the reader."

—Joe Lansdale,
author of *The Magic Wagon*

PEOPLE
OF THE
MESA

ARDATH MAYHAR

DIAMOND BOOKS, NEW YORK

To those who survived on the high mesa

PEOPLE OF THE MESA

A Diamond Book / published by arrangement
with the author

PRINTING HISTORY
Diamond edition/March 1992

ISBN: 1-55773-674-X

Diamond Books are published by
The Berkley Publishing Group,
200 Madison Avenue, New York, New York 10016.
The name "DIAMOND" and its logo are trademarks
belonging to Charter Communications, Inc.

PRINTED IN THE UNITED STATES OF AMERICA

10 9 8 7 6 5 4 3 2 1

FOREWORD

This is not history. It is an imagining of what might have been. After visiting Mesa Verde for the first time, in 1970, I found that the place haunted me. The mummified child I had seen in the museum popped into my mind often over the following years. I began to daydream about the place, the people who lived there, and the reasons they must have had for tackling the monstrous effort required to build in the cliff-sides.

A second visit in 1984 filled me with the feel of the place. As we drove down from the high mesa, chunks of material seemed to drop onto my head from the sky. Uhtatse—of course, he was the one who thought of building the cliff dwellings. The Ahye-tum-datsehe—in my imaginary past, that was what those people called themselves.

They were not much like the post-Columbian pueblo peoples, though there were things they had in common with them. And most of all, they were far different from the anthropological speculations mentioned in the many books written about them.

Instead of using the hypotheses of experts (who seldom have been farmers or have, indeed, lived at subsistence level on the edge of survival), I have used the discoveries they have made. The artifacts, the remains of buildings and tools and ornaments and pots, all the things they left for us to find, those tell more about the Anasazi as human beings than any amount of theorizing.

Having been a farmer all my life and having lived much of it in pretty primitive conditions, I feel that I can approach the subject with a different attitude. I understand the hard labor, sweat and blood, and gut-wrenching effort that challenge human flesh and bone and endurance. Perhaps, in this imagining of what the past might have been like, I may accidentally have hit upon some of the actual compulsions that motivated the Anasazi, when they lived on that high mesa, under skies that would not become those of Colorado for many centuries.

Nacogdoches, Texas
1992

The wind was cold. It whipped the leggings about his skinny shanks, set the trailing folds of his rabbit-fur blanket fluttering about his feet. It cut through to the middles of his frail bones, making them twinge with pain. He barely noticed the pain or the chill, however. He had spent his entire life ignoring such matters, and the habit was so ingrained now that it took no effort.

The sun was low atop the mesa across the canyon's width. Shadow filled the valley below the cliff on which he stood, and an eagle was circling, far beyond the range of his fogged vision. Yet he knew by the disturbance of the air and the feel of its living presence that it was there. His life had been spent in knowing such things. Even now, no living thing moved on or above or below the mesa that he did not recognize, note, and react to on some deep level of his being.

He was not sensing the eagle, however, or listening to the deer stirring in the oaks of the

Middle Way, set between the mesa top and the lowlands beneath the promontory. He looked down into the safe haven that his people had formed for themselves, sheltered snugly in the many visible crannies in the face of the cliff before him.

When the Tsununni came, fierce after many victories over other tribes, they found, inevitably, that the Ahye-tum-datsehe were no longer easy prey, trapped in their big stone towns atop the mesa. The battles fought there had taught his people something at last, and he had found the leverage to turn their old habits into new directions. It was the labor that gave meaning to his life. That thought filled him with satisfaction.

Now he had turned his long years of duty over to the nephew he had trained for that. He had no old wife sitting beside his fire to comfort his age. No one would stand beside his body and sing the death song when he went to join his fathers. He had none of the things that made age bearable, except for his memories, and they were wearing thin now.

The sharp scent of juniper moved about him, intensified by the cold wind. Suddenly, he felt light and young, as if he might be able to swoop out over the canyon as the swallows did in the freshness of a summer morning.

He had moved with them all his life, his senses meshing with theirs as they raced through the canyon-maze, seeing the flickers of

firelight in the big town and the smaller group-
ings of dwellings and single houses built into
cracks that seemed too small for anything but
the nest of a swallow. In his mind, he saw in its
entirety the complex of homes that he had
caused his people to build into the walls of the
mesa.

He perched on a stone and stared as the sun
halved itself on the horizon. It quartered itself,
and then it was gone amid a field of softest gold
and garnet. So many sunsets had played themselves out before his eyes . . . so many dawns, so
many nights of moon or of blackness.

The wind whipped more briskly through the
canyon, riffling the fur on his blanket. Below his
position, as the palest of glimmers, he could see
a lip of stone thrusting out over the sheer drop
into the valley. He recalled that stone with particular vividness . . . it reminded him of Ihyannah, his wife. That brought a twinge to his
heart, even after all the winters that had passed
since she had sat there, singing.

He was old. Until the task of smelling the
wind had passed to his successor, he had not
really admitted that or thought of it. But now he
knew, throughout himself. He was old, and his
usefulness was at an end. The vision that had
been his had passed to the young One Who
Smelled the Wind, and he could feel it draining
away from his body and his spirit as each day
passed.

Now, for the first time since he was a boy of

fourteen summers, he had the time to think of his life and the things it had brought to him and to the Ahye-tum-datsehe. The security of his childhood seemed almost a dream, now.

Only two or three of the oldest men and women of the tribe could recall, with him, those days when summers had been cooler, snow deeper in winter to provide water for the next year's crops, deer more numerous, and enemies distant and comparatively unthreatening. The younger ones could remember only the worsening weather and some few recalled the old enemy, the Kiyate, who had raided the dwellings on the top of the mesa. The newer enemy, never completely conquered, was one that everyone knew and feared.

The Kiyate were gone. Uhtatse wondered still where they had fled, when the Tsununni drove them away and took their place. It had been a bad trade. The Tsununni were not as easily discouraged from raiding as the Kiyate had been, although many years might pass between their forays. The infrequency of their raids was the only good thing about the change.

Now his kind was fairly safe from the incursions of enemies, but the weather was a thing that no man could change, and the gods seemed not to hear the chants that begged for a less cruel sun and more water.

Uhtatse had a bad feeling, deep in his bones, that matters for his people might alter for the worse, as the years went forward. In time, he thought with cold depression, they might have to go away entirely from the mesa that had been the home of the Ahye-tum-datsehe for as long as they had been a People.

Indeed, he had gone once to one of the Old Women to have her dream the future for him. Her dream had seemed like nonsense at the time, but now years had passed, generations of his kind had moved past his dimming gaze, and now he knew that she had seen a Truth, strange as it might seem.

To balance that vision, he had gone to one of the Old Men and asked for a dream of the past. Even anchored in tradition as that dream had been, it held matters that puzzled the younger Uhtatse and still filled him with bewilderment.

Now he stood at the edge of death. The matters of life and of time were stilled to a peculiar clarity.

Sitting in the worsening wind, he seemed to see down a long valley into the world of his youth. Every stone and leaf and incident of that valley's length came clear and immediate to his inner eye. When he turned his gaze in the opposite direction, he could see another valley stretching away, but there was a bend in its course. Beyond that, he could see nothing but a dim glow, as if a sun were rising there beyond his sight.

His feet were growing numb. Uhtatse knew that if he did not rise now and work his way down the cliff face into the shelter of the stone

*walls and the warmth of the fires, he would die
in the place where he now sat.*

*Yet why should he seek to live longer? He had
done the work for which he had been chosen, all
those many winters before. He had lived as is
fitting for One Who Smelled the Wind.*

*Why should he not die here on the lip of the
cliff, with the pinpoint glows of his people's fires
smiling at him from below and across the gorge?
His work was done, and now there was time to
retrace his steps, to see and understand what it
was that he had learned and been and accomplished.*

*The ancient closed his eyes, and tears from
the chill trickled down his cheeks. He didn't notice, for he was seeing into the past.*

II

Uhtatse sat motionless, legs and arms folded precisely as the Shaman had taught him. If the limbs were at rest, the mind could grasp the Teaching, the old man insisted. So the boy positioned himself and focused his mind upon Kishi-o-te's words.

"Not only the Kiyate threaten our people," the Shaman was saying. "There are other enemies in the low places, though they have not yet come into our country. We understand the Kiyate, and they us, and our battles are not terrible matters. Others may prove, in time to come, to be more difficult to deal with.

"Yet there are matters more immediate and more important to our survival. The rain must come, and the snow, or our crops will fail. The catchments must hold soil and moisture; the deer must thrive in the Middle Way, and the plants must grow on the mesa. For the deer to prosper, the oak leaves must be lush for browsing. The birds in the air and the growing things on our land must balance together, or we of the Ahye-tum-datsehe will suffer and perhaps will die." He looked sternly about at the six boys sitting before him.

"You are thinking that these are things that even a babe should know, and that is true. But not until you grasp a snake by the tail do you really take heed of his fangs. You must open your minds to the reality of what I am saying. You must let your thoughts play with all the things that might happen if any one of the matters upon which our lives depend should fail us." He stared at Uhtatse.

"What would occur if the snow did not fall in winter?"

Uhtatse shivered. "There would be no water in the catchment basins. We could grow very little in the gardens, for the rains are small and undependable. The small springs might dry up, and the deer would go away or die. We also would have to look far to find water and food."

Ki-shi-o-te nodded, a short jerk of his head. He turned his gaze toward Na-to-si. "And if the yucca sickened and died here on the mesa, what would happen?"

The boy's eyes widened. "There would be no long smooth cordage for bags and baskets and sandals. We would have nothing to clean with, for its soapy roots would wither and die. If the yucca died, we would do without many things."

The catechism went on from boy to boy, from

item to item, until all the necessary plants and creatures and phenomena of the mesa were tallied.

When it was done, Uhtatse felt anew the wonder he had felt at his first lessoning. So few things sustained their lives on the high mesas.

If the corn god turned his eyes away, if the rain and snow god grew angry, if any of the gods of any of the vital elements of their lives should be angered at the People, then all must perish or move to another place. And to move meant risking a meeting with the Kiyate, who ranged the rugged lands below the mesas.

A sharp breeze swept down the canyon, eddying about the stone outcrop on which the Teacher sat with his pupils. It held the first bite of winter, and Uhtatse wished that he had worn his turkey-feather blanket. But it was not permissible for discomfort to distract him. He straightened his back more rigidly and kept his gaze upon his teacher.

He was glad when this part of his day was done ... it was no easy thing to listen to the same words day after day. Vital as they were, they were boring, too.

The thing that devoured him with curiosity was the question as to what ability the Old Ones might find in him. What task would be set upon him, to perform all his life? He knew already that he was not a hunter, though he could provide adequately if it was necessary. He worked willingly in his mother's fields, but he had no feel for farming. His mother scolded him for dreaming or listening to the cries of birds while he was supposed to do things as simple as tending a fire or pulling weeds.

Yet the Teacher had chosen him, with six others, from all the other boys to hear the Teaching. From this rank would come a new Teacher, a new Healer, and a new One to smell the wind for change and for danger.

Three of their number would go back to the old tasks shared by all the members of the People. Uhtatse felt uneasily certain that he might be one of them. He felt inside himself no great aptitude for anything either ordinary or unusual. He seemed to be a gourd, hollowed out and ready for its content, yet still unaware what that might be. Yet he hoped, with the irrepressible confidence of youth, that they might find in him something he did not know was there.

On the day they were assigned to their life tasks, the Teacher handed Uhtatse a sleek feather from an eagle. "You will learn to smell the wind," he said. Uhtatse's heart leaped with fierce joy, though he knew that to be the most difficult of all the skills to learn.

He was not apprenticed to the old One Who Smelled the Wind. That was not the way in which one learned the delicate craft of sensing what took place on the mesa. Each person must find his own path to that sensitivity that noted everything, feared nothing, and could judge the meaning of anything he sensed, instantly and unerringly.

For Uhtatse, it meant that all day, every day, as well as for many nights, he must range the mesas, listening, looking, hearing-smelling-tasting the air, watching the movements of deer and kangaroo rats and chipmunks, of magpies and ravens and hawks and eagles. Every living thing must become a part of him.

As he moved silently through the thick growths of juniper and piñon, or lay silently in the fields of corn, or stood motionless on the lip of any of the stony edges of the cliffs, he was absorbing the things he needed to know through every one of his senses. Even the pores of his skin seemed to soak up the things he must learn. The mesa soon became as much a part of him as the faint thudding of his heart.

A day came when a hawk altered its pattern as it wheeled above him. Its skree came, but at the wrong time and in the wrong tone. A group of deer amid the serviceberry bushes flicked their large ears and disappeared into the brush.

Uhtatse, hidden in a runnel cut into the stone by melting snow, closed his eyes and felt. Smelled. Sensed.

The light breeze brought to his nostrils the tang of strange bodies. Men were coming, and not men of any people living on the mesa. Strangers! Strangers were approaching the high places.

He rose and slid through the junipers without a sound. The old One Who Smelled the Wind was waiting for him at the house of the Teacher's woman. Both smiled at the excited boy, as he gave them his news.

Ki-shi-o-te stared out over the fields toward the abrupt edge marking the drop to the Middle Way. "Warriors have gone to investigate those who come. But they are not Kiyate, Young One. These are the Anensi, who travel far and bring things for trading. You do not remember their last visit. Now you will meet with them, learn their sounds and smells, so that their coming will not disturb you the next time."

The Old One looked at him. "You have done well. I have watched you as you have gone about the mesa, down into the valleys, along the cliffs and down their faces. We are fortunate in you. When I am too old to serve my people, you will be able to do our work well."

The boy felt his face grow hot with pride, but he kept his expression solemn. To be praised by that one was an honor to be cherished. Perhaps the Shaman had known, after all, what he was doing when he chose Uhtatse to smell the wind.

III

The old men were turning away toward the circling junipers. Ki-shi-o-te led, his skin cloak draped in its most dignified folds. The Old Woman came from around the corner of the pueblo and greeted her peers before falling in behind him, and Uhtatse came last. In single file, the Teacher, the Seer, and the two Ones Who Smelled the Wind made their way along the paths to the spot where their way would intersect that of the approaching Anensi.

Uhtatse was aflame with curiosity. Except for glimpses of distant Kiyate, as they moved across the low country beneath the mesa, he had seen no outlanders since he was a tiny child, too small to notice the things he now wondered about. His memory was blurred, and only flashes of alien colors and scents came to him as he strained to recall that long-ago visit.

Filled with excitement, he yet managed to keep his face still, his motions dignified, so as to

make a match for the Elders. He took his place
with them at the Meeting of the Ways, where
others from the tribes living on other parts of
the joined mesas were already assembling.

There was an air of festivity about them.
Tonight there would be dancing on the roofs of
the kivas, feasts of venison and turkey and
hare, and long, long tale telling. He had heard
accounts of other visits of the Anensi, and even
the regular festivals for the weather gods did
not have the intense excitement these rare oc-
casions did.

Now he heard voices. Their tones were different, their words ringing strangely upon his ear,
the cadences alien to him. His nose twitched,
too, nostrils flaring. The scent that had come to
him on the breeze was stronger now, as the first
of the newcomers rounded the last steep rise of
the buttress rock. A dark face, much like the
faces of his own people and yet shaped with a
subtle difference, gazed upon those waiting
there. A dark hand rose in greeting.

The Healer had joined them quietly as they
waited. Now he and the Teacher, the Old
Woman Who Sang the Future, and the One
Who Smelled the Wind went forward together,
the trailing paws and tails of their fur robes
whipping in the brisk breeze. Four gray-haired
people, filled with cautious courtesy, moved to
greet these guests.

Uhtatse closed his eyes, thinking of a day
when he would make one of those elders, repre-

senting his part of the People of the high green mesa.

As the Anensi drew nearer, he saw that many were laden with hide-wrapped packs or with stick-and-fiber cages in which parakeets fluttered and small animals showed as furry lumps. Bags bulged heavily against the muscular shoulders bearing them. What exotic things might fill them?

He would have liked to join the rest of the children, who were now running forward, chattering questions at the patient traders. They felt the contours of packs and bags and poked their inquisitive fingers between the sticks of the cages, only to be nipped by irritable parrots or bitten by impatient beasts. One small one was already crying silently, great tears rolling down her round cheeks.

That was not the way for one who was to become the protector of his people to behave. Such childish things were now behind him, and he waited quietly, keeping his expression sober. Control of the self was the first of the matters he had learned from Ki-shi-o-te.

As the long string of walkers passed him, he watched everything. This was an entire tribe. There were old people and children, warriors and women and lads of his own age. Among those latter, he found one in particular who captured his attention.

This was a boy who walked proudly, his shoulders straight under the huge pack he carried. His eyes, too, were watchful, quick to note everything that came into their field. Those alert eyes met his as he stared. For an instant, something flashed between them, along their bonded gazes. Recognition? Impossible. But perhaps a certain kinship of spirit.

Uhtatse turned to follow the last of the Anensi toward the great Talking Place that his people had begun building on the edge of a commanding precipice. It was a long way, and he had the time to think, as he trudged along behind his excited people, of all the strange things he had encountered in the space of one short morning.

IV

It was indeed a busy evening. Fires bloomed about the Talking Place, as all the groups living on the mesa converged there to be near the traders. The Anensi camped together, the women putting together shelters of hide and pole with practiced ease, while the men squatted beside their opened bundles, bragging about their wares.

The smell of roasting meat filled the air, together with that of baking tubers and stewing vegetables from the gardens. Beans and squash simmered together in big jars to which red-hot stones were added from time to time to keep them at boiling heat.

The children, wild with the unfamiliar excitement, forgot their rigid training and ran about, getting into the ways of their mothers and being cuffed by their impatient fathers if they interrupted the haggling over the trade goods. It seemed strange to Uhtatse that those who possessed such a wealth of shell beads and woven goods and birds and salt and items for which he had not even a name might want or need anything the Ahye-tum-datsehe had to barter.

The pottery and the baskets, the dried foodstuffs, the carven wood pieces that were made in the winter seemed terribly familiar and valueless. He could not imagine their having any worth for others. But the Anensi had come a very long way for this trading. There must be things they wanted and needed, or they would not have troubled themselves with the harsh journey over harsher lands to get here.

That gave Uhtatse a different idea of his world. It held much that was not confined to the mesa top, it was evident. At times, as he lay upon one of the cut stones that still waited to be added to the Talking Place, he found himself dreaming of going away from the mesa, down to the lowlands with these people. He knew the Anensi were seldom troubled, even by the Kiyate or the Tsununni, for they traded with everyone. Even those distant and warlike people needed the things they brought from the east, the west, and the south. If he should go with them, he could see the world they were telling about, down there about the fires.

Listening with half his attention to the men talking just below his perch, he dreamed of the wide water they spoke about. That was a strange notion, he felt . . . water as far as one could see! In this arid world, that seemed almost impossible, and yet he did not doubt the words of the speaker.

And those cities of stone far to the south ... he would love to see how men went about building their own mesas and living inside them, instead of making low stone houses on the tops of the ground. Yet as he listened he found that he had no wish to see some of the ceremonies those people practiced. The words of the man below his stone perch made his skin crinkle, as they told of sacrifices of living men and women to the harsh gods of those distant ones.

A soft sound caught his attention. He turned his head to see the tall boy he had noticed earlier standing beside the stone, his dark gaze fixed upon him.

"You may come up here, if you like," said the young One Who Smelled the Wind.

With a nod, the other sprang up to land softly beside him on the boulder, whose surface was still warm from the sun. "You do not dance with the others," said the stranger. "You do not run with the young ones. You are, I think, one who is in training to be an Old One."

Such quick understanding was unusual, and Uhtatse warmed to the boy. "Yes. I have been chosen to learn to be the One Who Smells the Wind. I have been learning my craft for a year now."

"I thought as much. I, too, am in training and will be Shaman when the time comes. But I do not know about One Who Smells the Wind. What will your task be when the time comes?"

Uhtatse looked down into the fire below the stone, thinking how best to put words to his complex and unceasing task for one who did not understand what it might be. Carefully, he said, "We live here always, high above the lands below. All that threatens the People, besides wind and weather and predators, comes from the low country.

"Always, there is one who is tuned to the world about us so closely that he can feel at once any change ... in any *thing*. A strange presence crushing the grass or brushing through the oak trees of the Middle Way, a restlessness among the deer or the fowl of the air, a strange scent on the wind or a sound that does not belong in the world we know will serve as a warning to the one trained to know. He, in turn, warns the People.

"Our One Who Smells the Wind was one of those who met you as you came up the mesa. He is a great protector of the People. He knows even when the Kiyate move on the plains down there, for he can feel the troubling of the air where they go. He can smell the grease on their bodies over a great distance, and if they turn toward our place, we know and can prepare to defend ourselves."

The Anensi boy frowned. Then he smiled. "That is a skilled and valuable work, in a way not unlike that for which I am in training. I am Ra-onto. What do they call you?"

"Uhtatse."

Ra-onto made the sign for peace and friendship. Uhtatse did the same. Then, formalities done with, they lay together on the rock and looked down at the firelit scene below them.

"And are you a great hunter, as so many of your people are?" asked the Anensi.

Uhtatse grunted. "When I was a boy, my uncle taught me to use the atlatl and the spear, and I was not bad, if not good either. But now I cannot kill."

Ra-onto turned onto his side and stared at him, his dark eyes shining in the firelight. "You cannot kill? Not anything? Not even a rattlesnake or a tarantula in your blanket?"

"Nothing. I cannot pick a leaf from a tree or even crush a blade of grass, if I can avoid touching it. To do that is to divide myself from the world. If I did so, the mesa and the creatures on it would not speak to me, and I could not hear, even if they did. I cannot help my mother to pull the weeds from her gardens. I cannot pick a flower in the spring. Yet, in return, I can see and hear and feel things that it is not given to many to understand. It is a fair trade, I think."

Ra-onto nodded. "It seems to be. What can you feel now? Or is there too much noise and bustle here?"

Uhtatse had not tried sensing in such circumstances. It was an interesting thought, and he felt that he could try. He stared away from the fire, down into the darkness behind the great stone where he lay. He opened his ears, his nose, his heart to the words of the light breeze blowing chill across the mesa top.

He felt a great owl swoop to pounce upon an unwary mouse in the grainfield. A deer stirred, reaching for another nibble of oak leaves down in the Middle Way. The feel of the small herd around that individual came clearly to Uhtatse. A buck and two does and this single yearling.

Magpies quarreled softly in their roost. The water rippled in the wind across the catchments. Everything fitted together with seamless ease, nothing troubling the air or earth, the water or the creatures living in any of them.

"All is well," he said. "I had not tried doing that before. I am glad it can be done, even in the middle of such confusion. . . . It was as if my mind could close its door-hide, shutting out the light and the bustle."

The other boy looked impressed. "I can see that you do, indeed, have a rare gift. One that I would like to share, if that were possible. Yet, moving as we do, it would not work for us. Things must be familiar always for such magic to work its best."

As he thought about the words, Uhtatse found that he agreed. Amid ever-changing surroundings, one could never hope to find that attunement necessary for his work.

This made him realize how very different

must be the life that Ra-onto lived. He wondered, in turn, if the boy might not find the
mesa interesting. "Would you like to come tomorrow, with me? I will show you the mesa, as
very few ever know it."

Ra-onto's eyes brightened. "I would, indeed,
like to see your world through your eyes. I will
go."

Uhtatse rolled again onto his belly and
looked down at the men, still talking quietly of
things he would never see or smell or feel. But
he no longer had a desire to follow the Anensi
on their journeying. Something about the conversation with the boy at his side had given him
a new appreciation for his own place and people. It was as if he had seen them all, for an
instant, through the eyes of Ra-onto.

Now the chants that accompanied the distant
dancers sounded fresh to his ears. The pots
simmering beside the fires glowed with a new
beauty. The very texture of his turkey-feather
blanket almost felt unfamiliar to his fingers, as
he rolled the stuff between them, feeling the
twisted yucca fiber that caught bits of feather
in every winding, forming the fluffy warmth.
He had never thought of the way it was made,
even while watching his people form the
strands and weave them into cloth.

"I will show you the mesa," he murmured to
Ra-onto, "as you have shown it to me."

△△△△△△△△△△△△△△△△△△△△△△△△△△△△△△△△△△△△△△△

V

▽▽▽▽▽▽▽▽▽▽▽▽▽▽▽▽▽▽▽▽▽▽▽▽▽▽▽▽▽▽▽▽▽▽▽▽▽▽▽

The visit of the Anensi came with the first of summer. It enlivened the talk about the evening fires for many weeks, and the things for which the Ahye-tum-datsehe had traded were enjoyed for far longer than that. Among those matters were the parakeets that Ra-onto had traded to Uhtatse for his feather blanket.

That had been a hard choice to make. Uhtatse had been given the blanket by his mother, and he hated to lose it. Yet he traded at last and presented the birds to Ahyallah.

She was very pleased with his gift. The creatures' bright plumage and their shrill chatter filled her with joy as she twisted yucca fibers with fur or feathers for the men to weave into blankets. She kept their cage near, whether in her room in the pueblo, where she worked in winter, or outside beneath a big piñon, where she formed her fibers when the weather was fine.

She swore that the new blanket for her son would be a small price to pay for the pleasure she took in her new pets. And, indeed, it seemed that her fingers flew more swiftly to the accompaniment of the twitters of the parakeets.

It seemed to Uhtatse that he alone had been changed by the visit of the traders. Not only had he seen his own world with new eyes, but he had also been made aware that something was missing inside him, something necessary to his task of keeping his people safe. He felt, he smelled, he saw acutely, and he could interpret those sensations accurately. Yet he now knew that he lacked something vital, which had only now been revealed to him as he went about the mesa with Ra-onto.

The land itself did not speak directly to his heart, as it seemed to do for the old One Who Smelled the Wind. He had seen the man pause to bend over a plant, as if listening to some inaudible word it spoke. He had thought it strange and had not understood. Now he knew, with sudden certainty, that it was the plant and the soil in which it grew that spoke to the Elder.

The Old One heard what was spoken with no lips and said with no tongue. Uhtatse knew with equal certainty that he had never heard such words, not even after all his effort at sensing his world.

It was as if, in leading Ra-onto about the

mesa and pointing out the places where rabbits nested or magpies roosted or deer browsed, he had looked at those things with different eyes. He had recognized in them and in the trees and shrubs about him capacities that he had never attributed to any but men. With that new vision had come the understanding that he lacked the ability to know them.

It had troubled him ever since. He had gone to his elder and asked him for advice as soon as the problem was clear in his mind. The One Who Smelled the Wind had not been able to help him.

"Each of us must find the Way for himself, young one. For me it was as if a snowflake fell from the sky onto my head, opening my eyes and ears and heart to all things. It has been harder for you, as I have seen. Yet I cannot tell you how you must proceed from here. I believe that you will learn what is needful, however.

"You are perceptive, apt for the task in all other ways. Even as you stand, you will become a better than excellent Smeller of the Wind for the Ahye-tum-datsehe. If you can only achieve the higher perceptions, you will become such a master as we have not seen for many generations." The old man sighed and laid his hand on the boy's shoulder as if in apology. "It will come to you," he said, his voice hopeful.

So it was up to Uhtatse alone. He had suspected that might be true, from the beginning.

He was now forming a notion of the thing that might be hindering his search.

He had shed blood. Not since his childhood, it was true, and never since his training began. Even when he was being taught to hunt, he had not killed often, and yet it had been done, all those years ago. Now it seemed that the acts must be atoned.

He went to Ki-shi-o-te when he was certain of his course, and said, "I must purify myself. The shedding of blood, of rabbits and deer and birds, when I was young, is a barrier standing between me and the things I must learn. I must clean from my spirit all the small deaths that I have caused."

The old man looked into his eyes and nodded. "I will tell your mother. Go now, Uhtatse. Purify yourself and return, if the gods will have it so. And if we do not meet again, go with my affection. If you were my own nephew I could not feel more love for you. You have great potential for usefulness to our people. I hope strongly that you will survive and return to us."

He went away along the top of the mesa, avoiding the fields where his kin worked and the older pit houses, sunk into the earth, where a few of the people still lived. Shut into his own mind, he did not sense anything around him, but that did not mean that he stepped carelessly or injured anything that grew or crawled on the earth. Habit guided him safely amid the hazards of the way, and intuition took him far from the haunts of his kind to a point at which he could look away over long stretches of lowland.

It was a sharp cliff, thrust out into the space above the canyon below. The wind whistled between the teeth of rock that fluted its face, and the summer sun could not warm away the chill of the air. Not even a juniper grew near that perilous edge, as Uhtatse went over it, finding purchase with fingers and toes as he descended the sheer face.

He did not fear that a rotten bit of stone might collapse beneath his questing toe. Guided as he was, he knew that he was not meant to die at the foot of this precipice before he found the answer to his problem.

Some ten of his own lengths into the gorge, he found the spot toward which he had been impelled, as the shaft is cast from the atlatl when the hunter makes his throw. It was a shallow niche, just tall enough for him to stand. It was floored with sharp rock, which had pattered down over the years from the arch of sandstone overhead. It was too narrow for positioning the arms comfortably, and he was forced to hold them tight to his sides, hands folded over his belly.

In that terrible spot, thousands of feet above a tumble of deadly boulders and splits of stone, he settled himself to await his purification.

VI

The wind was sharp, even by day, and as the evening drew in and the sun moved below the farther edge of the high place, a chill breeze whipped through the canyons and about the spot where Uhtatse stood. His bare skin flinched into goose pimples, but he would not allow himself to shiver. He kept his arms in place, his legs steady under him, his teeth clenched tightly to stop their chattering.

His thoughts seemed to float away, high above his patient flesh. The cold was a thing he would not let into his consciousness. The hunger that soon growled in his belly was likewise rejected. The pain of standing on the sharp slivers of stone was so minor that it took no act of will to foreclose it from his mind.

Night hid the cliff across the gorge. Only its deeper blackness loomed against the stars, as bats moved above the cliffs and down into the canyons. He could hear the shrill screeches, though few of his kind seemed able to detect those almost inaudible cries.

The long cry of a hunting cat came to his ears, from down in the Middle Way where the deer browsed. An owl quartered the cliff-top skies above him. He could sense the downy beat of its wings. Somehow, in the darkness it was easier to sense all the hundreds of living creatures that shared the mesa with his own kind.

He concentrated fiercely, feeling for any whisper of the air among leaves and needles. He felt for the dim sensing of the yucca and even more humble plants. To know the living things, one must also know those that did not move or truly think. Yet their reactions could reveal many messages to one who could sense them.

It did not come in one night, nor yet in two, that ability he needed and sought. Uhtatse stood in the niche, his skin weathering like old wood, his mind soaring and searching among all the things living on the mesa and along its sides and in its streams.

As his belly flattened against his backbone and his ribs began to stand out like the ribs of the baskets his grandmother wove so well, his mind grew fat with another kind of food. Even had he been able to hear the words of plants and beasts unerringly, from the beginning, he knew that he would have been greatly improved by the things his stay on the cliffside was teaching him.

He forgot to count the days and the nights, as his spirit was drawn farther and farther away from his body. Such matters ceased to have any meaning, and he began feeling as if he might be a part of the wind moving about him, the light or the darkness wrapping around his body. A day came when he knew something of the stone against which he stood. It was a long patient tale of sun and wind and weather leading back to a time when water, wonder of wonders, lapped at it, and it was gritty stuff not yet hardened into the pale golden sandstone that he knew.

Realizing that he had heard the stone, he awoke from the trance that had held him for so long. He listened hard, and piñons whispered to junipers, which hissed back at them news of birds perching on their branches, sun warming their needles. He heard in his mind the small shriek of oak leaves being nipped away from their tree by the deer in the Middle Way.

Then he pulled himself back into his flesh. That was no easy thing, for a spirit that has known the freedom of the air does not willingly return to the burden of bone and muscle and nerve. As his mother twisted yucca fiber on a spindle, drawing into it bits of fur or feather, he spun himself back into his body. When he moved, at last, pain shot through every part of him.

He shook himself, squeezing his eyes shut. Then he opened them wide. Sparks of red and blue and white danced before his gaze until his eyes cleared and morning light shone steadily.

To move his hands and arms was very slow and terribly difficult. He took his time, flexing himself bit by bit, part by unwilling part. Now he felt that his body had grown light and seemed brittle. He felt as if he might step out of the niche and float like a dead leaf, lightly down into the canyon. But that, he knew, was caused by the long lack of food and water.

He did not trust himself to climb back to the cliff top until he was sure he could rely upon hands and fingers, feet and toes to do their work dependably. Even then, he moved slowly, taking great care with each hand and foothold. As he climbed, he felt the world winging through him in a thousand unfamiliar ways.

The wind spoke, as did the gritty stone beneath his fingers. When he reached the top and stood, facing back out over the dizzy deep, he shouted aloud the triumph of his spirit.

"Ho!" he cried, hearing the echo go bounding away along the canyons. He wanted to say more, to cry out to the morning his discovery of all this new world he was finding with every breath he drew. But he could find no words worthy to offer to those gods who had made him this gift. So he cried again, *"Ho!"* and heard the echoes wear themselves away among the stones.

And when he walked beside the corn plantings, he could hear the growing of the strong shoots in the sunlight. As plainly as those of his kind who worked among them, they spoke of well-being, of pain at being bruised, or joy at feeling water from the catch basins cooling their roots.

He must have been smiling broadly, for all who met him on the way began smiling in return when they saw his face. Ki-shi-o-te came from his house to greet Uhtatse, and Ahyallah forgot herself and sprang up from her stool beside her pile of yucca fibers to lay her hands on his shoulders. She had not done that since he was a boy.

Best of all—more than best, indeed!—was the reaction of Ihyannah, Ki-shi-o-te's daughter. She smiled as they passed on the trail.

That was better than food, better than being rubbed with oil and given clean clothing and his new blanket to sleep under. Indeed, once he stretched himself upon the hides of his sleeping place, that was the thing he dreamed of for hours and hours as the sun sank and rose again outside the pueblo.

VII

The old man sighed and shifted his weight on the stone. It was now fully dark. The last of the color had left the high layer of cloud lying along the east, and fires twinkled at him from the cliff homes across the canyon. In a strange way, he felt happier than he had felt in many years.

To remember Ihyannah always made him glow with the memory of warmth. Though she had, of course, been counted solely as the daughter of her mother, Sihala, she had been so much like Ki-shi-o-te that the old man had been much closer to her than was usual with fathers and daughters. Uhtatse had always known that they had the same clear vision of the world and their fellows. They had shared a feeling for the things that troubled the Ahye-tum-datsehe.

Because of his own closeness to the Teacher, Uhtatse had known an unusual harmony with Ihyannah, too. Sitting on the cold stone, he chuckled at the memory of his first gift to her.

Among the people of the mesa, nobody really needed a turkey. The fowls gabbled and dusted themselves and got underfoot and dashed blindly into the middle of anything that might offer food. Many thought them an unmitigated nuisance, though they were undoubtedly useful for their feathers and their meat. They came from the wild to settle among the People, who must have seemed to be inexhaustible sources of food.

Strangely, he had found it in him to love one of those ungainly birds. What had been its name?

In his youthful ignorance, he had thought that bird the most magnificent gift he could offer to her. Ah! To-ho-pe-pe! That was what he had called that turkey! To-ho-pe-pe.

Uhtatse chuckled softly, recalling the magnificent tail the bird had taken such pride in spreading as he swelled his chest and empurpled his ugly face. He had gobbled louder than any turkey ever known before. Ahyallah had considered him a burden that no family should have to endure, but she had said little. Uhtatse had been so solitary a boy that she was happy for him to have even so unlikely a companion as this one.

On the morning of his return, the bird had met him as he came back from his purification. To-ho-pe-pe had stomped about on the path before the key-shaped doorway of his mother's part of the pueblo, waiting for him. And when Uhtatse walked away toward Sihala's house, the bird followed, muttering and grumbling at his heels. It was as if the creature had missed him and was scolding him for leaving without any warning.

Other people had pets, of course, but those were rabbits and magpies that were caught and tamed, or parakeets traded for with the Anensi, or even, sometimes, puppies. Kangaroo rats and chipmunks were the pets of children. But only Uhtatse had a turkey. The laughter of his contemporaries had never bothered the boy, and it didn't bother him now. A friend was a friend, no matter if it had wattles hanging from its face and neck and terrible manners and worse habits. He was smiling as he listened to the constant mutter of turkey talk behind him.

Ki-shi-o-te was waiting in his wife's doorway, his face showing his gladness. They sat on the sunny side of the pueblo while Sihala moved back and forth with bags and baskets and cord, getting ready to store the vegetables as soon as they were harvested from the fields. She worried much, did Sihala, and much of her provender would spoil before winter came, but she never seemed to learn not to waste her time and strength.

Ihyannah sat on a stone, bent over her metate. Her grinding stone never faltered in its rhythm as Uhtatse approached, but he knew when she saw him. She went stiff for an instant, though her hand moved the *mano* without pause. Her dark eyes sparked as she turned to glance at him.

Neither spoke. That would be a breach of etiquette, for it was not fitting to show these emotions openly.

Squatting beside his teacher, the boy recounted the tale of his days in the niche. "Now I know," he said earnestly. "Now I feel and I hear the voices of all the living things and those that are seemingly lifeless, as well. The taint of that spilled blood has left my body and my spirit. I believe that now I can become the Old One that my people need."

The old man looked away over the lands far below the high spot where the pueblo stood. His eyes were bracketed with sad lines. "It is as well," he said, "for your predecessor has gone to the Place Beyond. Two days ago he disappeared. We have danced and sung for him, and his spirit has not spoken to us. He has gone from among us."

Uhtatse stared, shocked. "He was not ill . . . ," he began.

"No. It was the time for him. A stone he trusted broke beneath his foot. He fell from the cliff, and we have not found his body. That is where his spirit will be, grieving about the spot where his broken body is hidden. It will not be able to go to the Other Place, and that is a terrible thing."

Uhtatse rose. "I will find the place. I will

40

bring his body back, so that his bones can loose his spirit. He was my friend and the protector of our people. The grass will tell me where to look. The trees and bushes will reveal to me the spot where he lies.

"But before I go, I must ask you. Will your woman allow me to make a gift to her daughter?"

Ki-shi-o-te looked pleased. "You are now the One Who Smells the Wind," he said. "It would not be fitting for her to object, though you must ask her, of course. And also you must ask Ihyannah if such a gift would please her."

Uhtatse interrupted Sihala's constant going and coming by putting himself before her doorway, so she could not enter her house. "It would give me pleasure to make a gift to your child Ihyannah. Will you grant permission?"

Sihala was even older than her husband. Her eyes had faded to a pale golden shade, and she squinted with her effort to see him clearly. The wrinkled hands smoothed the basket they held nervously, as if they were uncomfortable when they were not busy.

"If my daughter is pleased, then I have no objection," she said, her voice thin with age and something like nervousness. "You must ask her. Ihyannah! You may leave your work."

The girl rose from her place, leaving the *mano* still warm from her hand amid the half-ground corn.

"What does the One Who Smells the Wind

want of me?" she asked. Her voice sounded meek, but her eyes were twinkling with laughter, and he could hear it in her voice as well.

That did not bother Uhtatse. Of all the young people on the mesa, only Ihyannah never laughed at him. She laughed at some secret inside herself that somehow she shared with him. He had always known that. And now the secret was coming out into the open, for when she looked deep into his eyes, he knew she had foreseen this day.

He smiled. "I have little to offer you, Ihyannah. Your mother is rich in blankets and food. Yet I have one friend in all the world. He thinks himself much greater than he is, but if you want him, he is yours.

"To-ho-pe-pe, this is your new mistress!"

Ihyannah leaned against the juniper that shaded the doorway and began to laugh. Even as she laughed, she held out her hand to the bird. A bit of meal clung to her fingers, and she let him pick it, though his beak must have hurt as he pecked.

"No one but Uhtatse would offer such a gift," she said, gasping. "I have been offered necklaces brought by the Anensi, birds with bright feathers, aprons of softest turkey feathers, but I have rejected them all. For what I wanted, truly and always, was a turkey of this exact size and temperament. A bird who knows his worth. Uhtatse's friend, as am I." She scratched the creature's ugly head, and he cocked his neck this way and that to let her reach the best spots for tickling.

The boy felt light, filled with joy and incredulity. Ihyannah was slim and strong, her thighs gleaming with oil, her small breasts just beginning to round into maturity. Her face was narrow and intelligent. Almost naked as she was, she glowed with the sunlight like the shells the Anensi brought from the distant sea, the light seeming to strike through her flesh. For such as she to wait for his gift was a wonderful thing, indeed.

He could not speak his feelings. He sought about in his mind for the proper words, but they were hidden in some cavern deep inside and would not come out for his use. Yet when she looked at him, he knew he need not tell her. She knew, and she had known for as long as he that they two were matched in their ways and their minds. It would be a good life, he knew.

"I must go now," he said. "I must find my old friend's body and bring it back. Think good thoughts for my search, Ihyannah." And that was his first use of her name, as his promised wife.

VIII

When he left the walled space before the pueblo, the breeze brought to him many signals. He paused before heading for the spot from which Ki-shi-o-te had told him the old protector of the People had fallen. Throwing back his head, he breathed to the depths of his lungs, sorting out the scents that came to him.

There seemed to be nothing but the odors of growing plants, animals of all kinds and sizes, birds going about their business, and people and their affairs. There was no taint of death in the air, though he would have caught that unmistakable scent, no matter how far he might be above the place where the body might lie.

He searched the sky for sign of a vulture, but only a high-circling hawk was visible, and distant eagles disturbed the air too far away to be of interest. Uhtatse moved along the edge of the cliff, cutting across promontories by perilous paths until he came at last to the edge where the old man had fallen. A broken stone outcrop, some yards down the cliff edge, showed fresh gray-gold edges. Below that, there lay a mass of oak scrub.

It would be safer, he knew very well, to go back and take an easier way down into the Middle Way. It would be very difficult to find the exact spot below, if he did that ... he must go down the sheer face, directly to the area just beneath the broken rock. It would be dangerous, he knew, but if the Old One's spirit was to go free, it must be done. Fresh from his ordeal, he had no fear now of anything the cliffs could offer.

Uhtatse felt that he could almost lean forward off the cliff to soar with a swallow's agility down to the Middle Way. He was still filled with exuberance, though he did not allow that to make him reckless. He worked his way down the face, finger hold and toehold, cranny and ledge, yard by yard. At last he found himself at a smooth face that offered no hold at all.

By then, he was only some five of his own lengths above the ground. There was a grassy patch onto which he could drop, so he pushed away from the stone and fell. He rolled easily and came upright again in the middle of the grass plot.

There was something that had troubled him since Ki-shi-o-te had told him of the older man's death. Why had he not sensed it as he waited in the cliffside? Surely, so momentous a death as this should have shouted itself into his perceptions. As he looked about the brushy space between himself and the cliff, Uhtatse grew more and more uneasy. Every leaf that was crushed in that fall should have cried out to him. Each swallow startled as the body plunged past its nest should have shrieked the news so loudly that he could hear.

Using every skill he had learned, the boy cast about for sign of a fallen weight. This near, even in the cool heights, there should be at least the beginning of the death smell. There was none. Branches should be broken, then, and leaves torn away. He would find that, if nothing more.

The morning wore away, and still he searched. The grass told him of sun and rain and snow, of worms burrowing beneath, but it spoke nothing about his mission. The breeze did not move at all, as if it held a secret not for his ears.

He stared upward at last, toward the bright fleck of broken stone high above him. It was barely discernible on the long courses of sandstone. Below it, and invisible from above, lay a shallow ledge, sloping toward his left.

That would have deflected the route of the falling man from a direct downward course. He moved in that direction, seeing and hearing and feeling with all his might.

And at last he heard something. Not the hiss of grasses beneath an unaccustomed weight.

Not the words of wind sighing over a shape that had not been there before. It was a human sound, soft and completely unexpected.

"Uhtatse . . . "

He jerked upright, staring ahead. Then he rushed forward, leaping a clump of serviceberry and plowing through a tangle of oak. Curled into a huddle beneath the thick branches was the one he had sought. Alive.

Quieting his heart and his breathing, the boy knelt beside the old man. "I have come for you," he said.

The dark eyes closed slowly, deliberately, and then opened again. "I knew . . . that you . . . would," came a breathy whisper in reply.

The question Uhtatse had been asking himself burst from his lips. "Why did I not feel you fall? Why did not the mesa tell me?"

He took the old man's hand between his own. "I was trying so hard to become what I need to be. And it seems that I have failed if I missed such a terrible event."

The hand moved in his. "I knew . . . where . . . you were. I did not want . . . for you to know. To come. I hushed it away from you. I knew how near . . . you were . . . to your goal. And now you have come. You have achieved . . . what you sought. I may die . . . at ease."

The eyes stared up as if trying to say something further that the lips could not utter. Then they went blank, and the hand was suddenly lax in his grip. The Old One was gone, and

Uhtatse was the One Who Smelled the Wind for the Ahye-tum-datsehe.

He blinked hard and straightened the frail body. He looked about for dead wood to fashion into a carrier, his gaze lingering longingly on the straight trunks of some of the young oaks. Yet that easy way was no longer for him. He had tried too hard, suffered too much to risk what he had gained, simply to make his task easier.

He found enough at last to shape a rough travois, such as the Anensi used to carry heavy burdens behind their bodies and those of their dogs. He tied it together with a part of the juniper bark cord he carried wrapped around his waist. When it was done, he rolled the old man's body onto the triangular vehicle and tugged at the pulling cords.

It was hard to move. He was still light from his long fast, and his predecessor was a big man, heavy in the bone, though his own flesh was worn away to nothing by his injuries and his long fast.

Uhtatse put his back into the task, leaning into the work of pulling his burden over the rough ground. Once he had it in motion, it moved more easily, bumping into holes and over tussocks.

It was a long way to the path that led to the top of the mesa. When he reached the place where he had to pause at the rock face, below the position of the watcher at that point, he stopped and set down the end of the travois.

A long call brought the watcher down to his level. Together, they pulled the long shape into the secret way that led around the obstacle to the cliff top. When they reached their goal, there was a man waiting for them. Ki-shi-o-te.

"I knew you would come," he said, just as the Old One had done. "Welcome home, Smeller of the Wind. We shall attend to our brother's body now. You may go to your rest, for you have proven yourself equal to the task with which we must burden you."

Uhtatse looked down at the limp form on the travois. He stared up into Ki-shi-o-te's eyes. Then he turned his steps toward his mother's house.

Tomorrow he would become, in every way, a man.

IX

He did not seek out Ihyannah. He turned his steps away from the house where Ki-shi-o-te lived and veered away from the path to his mother's doorway. This was a time when not even those who were nearest to him could be of help. He knew he must accept his new responsibilities now, making them a part of himself.

That could only be done alone, and the time was short. Morning would find him standing on the point of rock where all his predecessors had stood to assume their terrible duties.

Still weak from his long fast, he sought out a spot among the junipers that was sheltered from the sharp breeze that had risen just after he found his mentor. Lying amid the prickly vegetation, he stared up into the cloud-streaked sky.

A magpie alighted on a brittle branch and cocked its head to look down at him. Its immaculate white and black feathers gleamed in the fitful sunlight, and it seemed to be studying him.

Rough juniper bark was grasped in the tough claws ... he could feel it plainly. Wind riffled feathers along the back and the edges of the wings. The bird was curious, alert yet intrigued.

Uhtatse felt deeply into the creature, to find that it was trusting him, knowing him to be unlike those of his kind who flung stones or cast short spears from the atlatl to kill any creature that could be boiled for broth. It knew!

Filled with emotion, he opened his eyes and looked up into those berry-bright orbs so near his own. It, too, trusted him to keep the mesa safe. The birds, the deer, the chipmunks and hares, the turkeys and dogs, and all the varied creatures knew him. Not only the People depended upon his skills, it seemed.

It was a sobering thought, and he took it with him through that dream-filled day and the overcast night that followed. When he rose with first light and went to his mother's house, he knew things that he had not learned in any way he knew. He understood matters that no other of his kind, excepting only Ki-shi-o-te and the Healer and the Seer, comprehended.

The mesa was not a thing for mankind alone. It was a circle, and his own kind had a place inside it. But all the creatures, the plants, the stones, even, had their own places there, too. If one disrupted that circle, all would suffer. It was his task to see that the circle was never broken at any of its links, to sense if any danger threatened its integrity.

One who had not purified himself, learning to hear the voices that were too small for normal ears, could not be a powerful One Who Smelled the Wind. He had known that before, but now he understood it completely.

He rose and turned toward his mother's part of the pueblo. It was time to prepare for his acceptance into his new position.

As his mother combed prickles from his hair with her brush made of fine rootlets, he stood very still. Even when she pulled, he didn't protest. His sisters were brushing the deer-hide robe they had decorated with beads and quills when he was first chosen to be trained for his position. He didn't object now when they turned him around to try it about his shoulders.

He understood them, as well as the magpie and the beasts and rocks and plants. They were glad for him, and he felt their affection like the warmth of small flames licking about his spirit.

When the sun was above the rim on the east, he was ready. His sandals were on his feet, the stiff texture of the decorated yucca fiber tickling his soles. His robe was arranged carefully, his headband tied with great care by his mother's hands.

He thought, just for an instant, of his uncle, who would have been very pleased, had he lived until this day. Then the thought slid away as they went out and down the path toward the promontory where he would accept his life's work from the hands of Ki-shi-o-te.

X

When he moved out onto the narrow tooth of rock, extending over the depth of the canyon, he felt it quiver slightly beneath his sandals. With sudden clarity, it came to him that he would be the last One Who Smelled the Wind to take his place here, receiving his charge from the Shaman of the Ahye-tum-datsehe.

This stone would fall, in time, into the valley below, leaving a gash where it had been. The Old One had met his death that way, and the rock would follow him, in time. The thought did not make Uhtatse's feet unsteady as they paced the length of the projecting boulder.

At the very end, he stood looking into the eye of the sun, which now sat a hand's breadth above the eastern rim of the canyon. It filled his eyes with pink dawn light, and he turned to face those waiting on the mesa behind him. Step by step, with great dignity, he returned along the span, the stone vibrating subtly at every step.

Ki-shi-o-te met him as he stepped onto the flat stone forming the base of the platform. His wrinkled face expressionless, he laid a long, polished staff on Uhtatse's outstretched hand. It was of oak, straight and strong, well cured. It had been peeled when fresh, and long years of wear had rubbed it to a rich luster. It was the staff borne by every One Who Smelled the Wind for many generations.

Ihyannah came forward with a necklace in her slender hands. It was made of feathers and carved bone, claws of hawks and eagles, teeth of big cats. Strung on juniper cord, it bound its wearer to every part of the mesa.

She handed the thing to her father, and Uhtatse bent his neck to allow the old man to slip it over his head and arrange it on his shoulders. He would, he knew, never wear it again, but this once was enough to infuse into him all the accumulated wisdom of those who had worn it over the years. His skin warmed where the sacred necklace touched him, and he felt an instant of union with everything alive.

When Ki-shi-o-te and his daughter drew back into the group, Uhtatse could see his shadow drawn in ocher and purple on the sandstone before him. He lifted the staff at arm's length above his head. As it moved, a brisk wind swept down the canyon, riffling the necklace feathers at his neck and fluttering the tail of his headband across his ear. High above, a hawk shrilled twice.

Down in the still-shadowy depths of the canyon, the swallows were wheeling and dipping, burbling their morning cries. Even as he stepped from the rock onto the soil of the mesa, he had a sudden dizzy vision.

It was blurred and unfocused, but he seemed to see people moving up and down the steep cliffs, bearing stone and juniper posts. Building, down there in the deeps—what? There came a swirling vision of pueblos in the cliffsides . . . and then he shook his head and was steady again, seeing nothing but the sandstone cliffs, with their arched openings, before his eyes.

Sihala stepped forward, holding in her hand a basket filled with shelled corn. She handed it to him, turning her head politely so as not to meet his eyes. She beckoned to Ihyannah, who moved forward a single pace and stood looking up at Uhtatse.

To-ho-pe-pe gabbled importantly and bustled forward between the feet and legs of the onlookers to join his mistress. Uhtatse felt a terrible impulse to laugh, but he controlled it and avoided looking at Ihyannah. If they looked into each other's eyes, they would both break into laughter, and that would not be fitting at such a solemn moment.

He reached to take her fingers into his own.

The two of them went down the path toward Sihala's home, where Ihyannah would stay for a while. When the harvest was in, they would hope to build a room onto the pueblo for themselves, or they might even make a pit house. For now, they must remain with their parents.

He knew that she would help him to remove his robe and necklace and lay them away in the basket where they were kept, along with the staff. The two of them would work silently, speaking no word but communicating with their hearts.

It had been a strange day, a breaking-away from all his life before this. It was frightening, exhilarating, and stimulating, all in one. He smiled at Ihyannah.

She glanced back to make certain that they were out of sight of the rest. Then she smiled back.

To-ho-pe-pe came after them, wings spread, chest expanded to its fullest roundness, wattles at their most astonishing shade of purple. As he caught up to them, he paused to dance in a circle, gobbling mightily all the while and trailing his wing tips in the dust of the path in an eccentric pattern.

Ihyannah began to shake. Uhtatse felt his own rib cage begin to quiver.

Laughing, they went down the path together, hands clasped. The turkey followed them, doing its war dance and raising echoes across the canyon with its raucous comments.

The old man sitting on the cliff felt a sympathetic chuckle rising within him. That had been a good day. Not the best of all that were to come, perhaps, but a good day, filled with happiness. He and Ihyannah had shared something very rare and precious. It had ended, of course, as all things must end for those who walked in flesh, but the memory had warmed him for many seasons.

Yes, it had ended as the life on top of the mesa had ended, when the time came. He had been the one who caused that, to be sure, and he could not regret it. His own life, indeed, was about to end. He could not regret that, either. It was fitting, and that was a good thing.

XI

The mesa had not changed. The people and the dogs, the birds and beasts and plants seemed to be just as they had been all Uhtatse's life. From his earliest memory, little had altered on the high mesas.

Yet something had changed. He had changed, permanently and drastically. The mantle of responsibility that had hung about his shoulders as he stood on the quivering rock of the promontory might have been laid away in its basket, but the reality of the task it had bestowed upon him was never absent from his mind.

He slept little. It was summer, and that was the time when the enemy would come, if the Kiyate came at all. The most worrying thing about those fierce people was their randomness. Years might pass without an incursion, and still they might hit the vulnerable pueblos at any time. He had to be watchful, day and night.

It would have helped to have the comfort of his own home and Ihyannah, but their true marriage would only take place when they moved into the part of the pueblo that would be Ihyannah's. Until then, they could take pleasure in one another, talk and laugh when there was time, and walk away into the junipers to make love. But they could not live in the same house or eat from the same pot. They could not reach out in the night to comfort each other's nightmares.

Those nightmares, for Uhtatse, were becoming regular visitors. He would wake, sweating, on his bed pile. Not until he rose and went out into the night, walking fast and breathing deeply, would he shake away the miasma of the dream. And yet he could seldom recall the substance of that dream ... what was it that was haunting him in the night?

When he began to awaken others in his mother's house, he took to sleeping outside amid the piñons clumped together beyond the pueblo. It was chilly once the sun set, but he rolled into his feather blanket and tried to sleep. The dreams became worse, not better.

The restlessness of his dreaming sent him moving about the mesa at all hours. Even in the darkest time of the night, he would roam up and down the slotted rims of the mesas, feeling afar for any disturbance. More and more, he believed that there was danger out there in the lower country, moving nearer and nearer as day followed day.

It would have helped if he could have wearied himself with hard work in the gardens or with the hunters. Yet now he was committed, and it was impossible for him to distract himself with those necessary labors. Others must do those things, while he sent his senses frantically across the mesas and over the lands below.

He said nothing to Ihyannah. Her laughter was precious to him, and he would do nothing to damp her high spirits. Indeed, only her cheerful heart and her warm, responsive body made life bearable for him as the summer bloomed and faded.

His wife, however, was sensitive as well as intelligent. He lost weight and became abstracted. That was not lost on her, and she came at last to touch his shoulder.

"You are troubled, Uhtatse. All is well on the mesa. There is no sickness. The gardens flourish. The game is fat and the weather excellent. The thing that troubles you comes from inside, not from outside. It will make you ill if you keep wandering in the night and worrying about whatever is down there in the low country.

"It would help if we could live in the same house, and yet the building of the new space is not complete. It is forbidden to move into rooms that have not been purified and had the ceremonies performed to make them wholesome. If you will allow me, I will move out into the piñons with you."

He turned to lay his cheek against the top of her sleek head. She smelled like earth and air and juniper. That comforted him on some deep level of his being.

"I feel as if the weight of the mesa rests on my shoulders," he said. "I worry that some enemy will creep up and I will not know. I am responsible for the safety of our people, and I feel that I am not old enough—or skilled enough—to keep them safe." He sighed. "Ki-shi-o-te tells me that this is natural. No one, however skilled, he says, can keep anyone safe, for our world is not a safe place. And yet I cannot rest, and I dream . . . "

"We will build our own house," said Ihyannah, aware that she was saying something unheard of.

Uhtatse drew away to look down at her, his eyes wide. "It is forbidden to build on the mesa, except in the prescribed ways. And a pit house would take more time to dig than I can spare from my work, besides being cramped and stuffy." He tightened his arms about her, staring away across the canyon.

He found his gaze lingering on the deep arch that opened into the side of the cliff beyond the gulf of space. A cave. He had explored it when he was small. It was deep and cool, with a spring seeping from the stone in its deepest part. There were others like it along all the cliffs on both sides of the canyon.

He had a sudden recollection of the words of the Anensi trader. Those tales of cliffs that the people of the south built for themselves and within which they lived.

A house built into the cliff cavern would be cool in summer and warm in winter, shielded from the blasting winds that swept the high places. It would be safe, also, from enemies, who would have to negotiate the almost-impossible climb down to it.

"The cliff," he breathed. "We could build a house inside the cliff. That would break no rule."

Ihyannah pulled free to stare into his face. "In the cliff? How?"

"Look over there, at that small cave. There are others below us here, large ones and small. Most of them have little springs seeping from the stone, too. We could build a house there, and it would not be on the mesa. The ritual would not have to be performed for an entire house. We could live there until our part of the pueblo is finished."

For the first time in weeks, he looked animated. There was a coppery glow beneath his dark skin. His eyes were bright, instead of harried.

Ihyannah turned to lie on her belly and stare down the cliffside. "There is a cave just below us. I used to play there when I was small. It does have a spring . . . yet it is a long way down. It is not easy to get there, though I thought little of it when I was a child."

Uhtatse sank back into her arms, his cheek again against her hair. "It would be a very difficult thing. Dangerous, too. We would have to do it all ourselves, for there is no one else who can spare the time or take the risks." He frowned. "And I must watch the mesa. How can that be managed?"

She laughed, shaking in his arms. "We will go on a long scout. Down past the Middle Way to the very bottom of the mesa. We will move across those distant lands below, and you can sense everything that moves. If it takes days, then we will take those days. When we return, you will know that there is no trace of the Kiyate anywhere within range of us.

"Then we will begin to build my house. If we work for half the day and you range the mesa for the other half of every day, then all will be done. Nothing will be neglected."

Uhtatse felt his spirits rise. For the first time since he had held his position, he felt some ease of mind. The dark mouth of the cave smiled at him. A magpie above his head shrilled an inquiring note, and he looked up to smile at the bird.

Something was trying to speak to him. Something inside struggled to make itself heard. If he was patient, he would know, eventually, what it was.

XII

It would never have occurred to Uhtatse that scouting the lowlands might be sheer pleasure. He had, of course, gone there with the Teacher as well as with his uncle in order to learn the country. That was as necessary as knowing his own high mesas.

Yet those forays had been focused on other purposes: spotting likely places for an ambush, finding springs or creeks that could provide water for any who came against them, or locating points at which watchers might be stationed in times of severe danger.

But now Ihyannah was with him, and the land they crossed was turned into a magical country, filled with wonders. As she moved quietly and skillfully through the brush and the grasses, she noted everything with different eyes from his own. He found himself joining her as she admired dusty blossoms, odd-shaped stones, bushes that looked like beasts or men.

Through her perceptions, the scout became sheer pleasure, and Uhtatse began to have a dim understanding of the reasons why women so often looked with patient contempt upon the blindness of men.

They were also alone for the days it took for them to make a wide circle, testing the wind, checking for tracks, feeling the earth for the presence of an enemy. While they seriously and steadfastly did all those things, they also laughed far more than would have been seemly if there had been others to hear them.

They ranged far, noted everything. They found nothing at all threatening. When the long-range scout was completed, they began their house building, working every afternoon after Uhtatse had checked out the mesa.

It was brutal work. Cutting the sandstone into shape was long toil, using the bone and stone tools available to them. They worked together, sitting in the scanty shadow of junipers or toiling side by side in the thin, hot sun. Working in gritty harmony, they shaped the building blocks of their house, and many who found an idle moment came and helped them, though all showed signs of wariness. The thing they were doing was outside all their traditions, which made it somewhat suspect.

The more difficult part of the task was that of getting the cut stones down the cliffside and into the cranny they had chosen. Many had suggestions as to the best method of carrying the blocks down to the ledge, but nobody volunteered to demonstrate.

After trying one descent, burdened with a stone that had been slung from his forehead by a tumpline, Uhtatse knew that something else would have to be devised; the weight of the stone hanging on his back unbalanced him dangerously as he negotiated the perilous way downward. He knew that no matter how many safe descents he and Ihyannah made, sooner or later that weight would overbalance one of them and pull the unfortunate victim over the cliff.

He took the problem to Ki-shi-o-te, who had watched the efforts of his daughter and her man with great interest. He was one who, no matter how old and traditional he might seem, always noted and appreciated new things. He was, of course, entirely too feeble now to give physical help, but he had lived long and noted much. His advice and experience would be valuable. He made several suggestions, but none of them really helped much.

By the time all the stones were cut for the tiny shelter, along with enough juniper poles to hold up its roof, the young people were almost at their wits' end. The best notion, so far, was that of letting the stones down over the lip of the cliff, to be caught by someone positioned in the cave with a long pole, which could hook the cord and swing the block into the arched opening. But the juniper-fiber rope kept breaking, allowing the painfully shaped stones to fall into the canyon.

Ki-shi-o-te had been the nephew of a weaver. He knew the comparative strengths of different sorts of materials, and he put his mind to the problem. There was a need for something to strengthen their ropes far past normal needs of his people.

At last, he came up with an ingenious mixture of ligament from game, hair from the ubiquitous dogs, and juniper fiber, all twisted into thin cords, which were, in turn, twisted together to form heavier ones. When the desired thickness was gained, yucca fiber was wrapped about the rope from one end to the other. "If anything will bear the weight of the blocks, this should do it," he said when he had in his hands the first rope of the new sort.

Uhtatse was sitting in the shadow of the wall, watching Ihyannah grind meal for her mother. He was wishing this was his own woman's house and that Ihyannah was grinding the meal for them. He wished even more fervently that when the sun went down, they could go together into the doorway of his woman's house.

He looked over at Ki-shi-o-te. "Do you think this will do what I want?" he asked.

The old man fingered the strong strand. "It should. But the task of making your rope is going to be as difficult as that of shaping your stones."

He was right. Their hands, sore and scraped from stonecutting, were now further abused as they gathered the materials and twisted strands into cords, and cords into ropes. By the time they reached the last step, wrapping the yucca fibers about the ropes, their fingers were raw, and they left stains of blood on the strands.

Their ropes held. The golden-tan blocks began going down into the cliffside as Uhtatse fastened the blocks with the rope, slipping the strands into grooves cut for that purpose. He lowered away, using a juniper stump for a belaying point, while Ihyannah, below in the cave, reached with her crooked pole and brought the blocks into the arch.

They piled up satisfactorily, and at last the pair realized they must begin building, or the available space for working would be too cluttered to allow them to move about. The walls began to rise.

The Ahye-tum-datsehe were very interested in this new sort of construction. New things were always fascinating and seldom found on the top of the mesa. From time to time a neighbor or relative would volunteer to help with the building after the work of the day was done. So the house went up far more quickly than anyone had thought it might.

It was, of course, very small. Hardly larger than one of the scorned pit houses, it held one big room with benches built around all the walls. The spaces beneath them would hold tools and hides and winter food stores. The fire pit was carefully located so as to take advantage of the ventilating hole in the roof, and Ki-shi-o-te himself crept down the cliff to drill the *sipapu* that would give them access to the spirits beneath the earth.

A smaller room was for stocks of wood and cordage, hides too large for the bench-cupboards, and all sorts of pots and jars that would not fit easily into the living space. That was built last, and when it was shaped, they began chinking the cracks with mud.

Uhtatse smoothed the gritty mud into a crevice with his thumb and looked up at Na-to-si, his old friend, who was completing the brush layer on the roof. "If many people wanted to build in this way, it would be a good thing to have builders working in the caves as the stones came down. There would not be the clutter of stones at first. And they could put them where they wanted them without having to handle them twice."

"An interesting thought," Na-to-si replied. "Have you noticed how cool it is here, even though the sun is burning onto the top of the mesa? It should be easy to keep warm here in the winter, too. The wind comes from the other side of the mesa, and you will be sheltered here in the cliff. The sun will slant back beneath the overhang then as well. The pueblos are well and solidly built, but the wind whips past the hide door coverings and through the rooms and down the smoke holes."

He put the last of the roof into place and leaped down beside Uhtatse. "It may be that when the new part of the pueblo is finished and cleansed, you and Ihyannah may not want to return there from your little house down here. It is noisy up there in the cold weather."

Uhtatse laughed. He had had the same thought. Here alone, without the constant buzz of activity in the large complex, it would be very quiet and private. He moved through the doorway and looked over the edge into the canyon.

"Children would fall over here," he said. His tone was doubtful. "It would be dangerous for small ones."

Na-to-si glanced down and shrugged. "I will build you a wall, if you decide to remain here. Then the small ones cannot go toddling over the edge."

They laughed together. Neither believed that one of the Ahye-tum-datsehe would willingly live apart from his fellows for longer than was absolutely necessary.

The old man sitting on the cliff top sighed into the darkness. It had been a long time ago. So much had happened since!

That wall . . . even if Na-to-si had built it, it would not have saved his child. The thought of that small one was still a pain inside him, though of course he concealed it. It was the part of an uncle, not a father, to grieve for, to train, and to love children. Yet that pain nested inside him, beside that other pain that always accompanied the thought of Ihyannah.

Yet along with the pain there was also satisfaction. There had been danger and hardship, as always. Not one of the Ahye-tum-datsehe would know how to live without those things as a constant companion of living. And yet he had done much in his overlong life.

Uhtatse clutched his robe closer about his shoulders and tucked his feet beneath its trailing edge. It was so cold now. It reminded him of the first winter after his marriage.

That had been the first of a long series of harsh winters that stayed far longer than usual upon the mesa. The weather's change had brought other changes, too, and his people had had to learn new ways to survive in their old home place. He liked to think that he had helped them to do that. Perhaps . . . perhaps more than any other of his tribe.

XIII

When the house was finished, the ritual done that made it fit for the People to inhabit, Ihyannah seemed very pleased. Uhtatse himself, though he knew it belonged solely to his new wife, felt pleasure when he looked at the smooth stone floor and the fire pit, the benches and the skins covering them.

Not for the first time he thought how pleasant it would be to be away from the squeals of children, the clacking of parrots, and the constant growling and fighting of dogs.

The building on the pueblo itself had gone more slowly than usual. It would be months yet before the new section would be completed. Here they could live together in peace, away from the demands of the larger dwelling. But even as they smiled at each other, there came the sound of hands and feet that scraped at the cliff face. They were about to have their first guest.

Na-to-si swung around the breast of stone siding their cranny. He landed softly on the shelf of rock as they stepped out to greet him. On his back was tied a fiber bag, and he laid that on the ledge to open it.

Inside was a finely worked deer hide, which Na-to-si presented to Ihyannah.

"This will warm you at night," he said. "My mother honors the woman of the One Who Smells the Wind."

Uhtatse reached to touch the soft hide. It was a fine piece of work, made with love, and he was touched.

Ihyannah spoke for him when she said, "You must bring her to see my house."

The young man shook his head. "She could not climb down the cliff. She wishes you well, but she cannot visit you. All wish you well, in fact, and many envy you your quiet nest here."

That was the first of many gifts. Pots and jars, baskets and bags, bowls and spoons arrived, all made with painful effort and ornamented with the best designs the Ahye-tum-datsehe had yet contrived. Such gifts freed the new wife to begin making her own garden plot, twisting her own cordage, making her own house livable for the winter. They meant, as well, some sacrifice, on the part of the givers, of the time they had to contribute to the well-being of their own families.

The summer passed quickly. Uhtatse, busy about his duties on the mesa, watched the leaves turn, the burrowing animals dig deep, the migratory birds pass over early and in dense ranks. Every instinct he had told him that this would be a harsh winter.

He passed the word to his people, but they had already felt the same message in their bones. They had done all they could do, and a wealth of hides and jerked meat, of grains and squashes and beans crowded the storage places and even edged into the living space of the People.

At night, the men danced on the roofs of the kivas, while the women swayed in circles about them, chanting the song to the wind and the snow and the weary sun. In every way they knew, they did the things that might ensure their survival in the coming season.

When the snow came, it was heavy and seemed never to end. Uhtatse, whose work did not end as that of the hunters and gardeners did, found himself dreading the coming of day, when he must leave the pile of hides and furs where he slept with Ihyannah in a warm huddle.

She rose when he did, helping him into his leggings and winter moccasins and the cloak of hide lined with rabbit fur that his mother had made for him. She forced him to eat a bit of the fermented corn mush or a strip of meat from the jar of jerky. He begrudged taking the time, but they both knew that the cold is a subtle enemy that can drain away the strength from one who dares to face it ill nourished.

The climb of the stone face was dreadful. It was often slick with ice, treacherous with riffles of snow along the finger and toeholds. He learned many useful lessons about moving on icy rock, the most valuable of which was to string a strong rope of yucca fiber twisted with tendon between the bottom and the top of his precipitous ladder. Ihyannah tied knots at intervals to give secure handholds, and once that was in place it didn't matter if he slipped from his foothold. The rope saved him from many a fatal fall.

The surface of the mesa was still and strange beneath the thick layer of snow. Few animals moved, even in their deep burrows. Only deer browsed in the Middle Way, digging with their sharp hooves through the crusted drifts in order to reach patches of long, dry grass.

Uhtatse woke one morning in midwinter with the feeling that it was futile to keep prowling the mesa. In such weather, no enemy would or could come. Other storms could not take his people by surprise, for this winter they expected nothing else. Why did he continue quartering the difficult terrain, freezing in the sleet-ridden gusts from the northwest?

Even Ki-shi-o-te asked him why he did not remain indoors in such terrible weather. "What can you learn that we do not know already?" the old man inquired. "You will slip from the edge of the mesa or freeze yourself into stone, and that will leave Ihyannah a widow. Care for yourself, Uhtatse."

But he was too young and restless to spend the days in the kiva with the men, playing their endless games with pebbles on marked hides, weaving the cords that the women twisted into fur blankets, or chewing the potent bud for which they traded with the Anensi. Ihyannah would make love for only so long, too, without pushing him from her house, saying that she must do her work.

He had no other task, as the rest of the men did. He didn't carve bone into small beasts and decorative shapes or weave blankets or make beautiful bowls out of burls of the juniper wood.

No, he had only one sort of task, and he was not at ease unless he was about it. He sighed heavily. Ihyannah opened one eye and then uncovered her face.

"There is venison for you, and I boiled dried squash and beans enough to last for days. Do eat enough, Uhtatse. I hear the sleet rattling on the stone, even here in my house in a cave." She sat and pulled her deerskin winter dress over her head.

"You will need two sets of moccasins today and two pairs of leggings. I can feel the bite of the wind, even sheltered as we are by the cliff. It must be bitter on the top of the mesa." She rose and bustled about the small room, folding away their sleeping skins and putting his food on a clean split of wood.

He finished lacing the leggings about his chilled shanks, pulled on his heavy cloak, and turned to her. She put her arms about him and held him tightly. They stood together for a long moment, delighting in the touch of flesh and the delicate contact of emotions and thoughts that accompanied it.

Then he ate hurriedly. It was day outside the door-skin, as he could see through the slits at its edges. It was time he was at his work. The mesa waited, huge and cold and lonely, for only he kept it company on such mornings.

He moved up the face cautiously. Sleet made the rock terribly slick.

He turned to call back down to Ihyannah, who watched anxiously as he went. "Be very careful if you go up today. Even with the rope, it is not safe. Your mother will know why you do not come."

But he knew she would go, anyway. Such small things as weather and ice did not stop Ihyannah from doing what she thought necessary. Her mother was ill now, and Ihyannah cooked and did the small tasks necessary to keep her mother and father comfortable in the cold weather. She would be carrying wood to stack beside their door for much of the day, he knew. He did not begrudge that, for Ki-shi-o-te was like an uncle to him, now that his own uncle was dead.

He was moving with great care. His fingers gripped firmly. His toes nudged deeply into the crevices before he loosed any previous hold. The rope hung between elbow and side, ready to be clamped quickly if needed.

It jerked crazily, and he stopped. There came a thud from below, and a moan of pain.

"Ihyannah!" He slid recklessly down the strand, knowing that she must have begun her climb and fallen.

Luckily, she had not been so high up that their shelving outcrop had not caught her as she came down. She was drawn into a knot when he reached her, knees against her chest. She made no sound, but he saw the mark of pain on her face.

"Are you all right?" he asked, dropping to his knees beside her.

Then he saw the bright blood creeping onto the stone and freezing there. It came from beneath her skirt, and he felt a chill of apprehension.

"Take me to the House of Women," she gasped. Her fingers were bloodless with the pressure of her grip on the stone beside her.

Shivering with something too much like fear for comfort, Uhtatse went into the house and brought out a thick fur blanket. He wrapped it about her and tied the rope beneath her arms, placing her directly below the stone stair.

When he reached the top, he gave the long

hail that brought help to any of his people. Na-to-si was beside him very soon.

"Ihyannah has hurt herself. She must go to the House of Women. Help me to draw her up the cliff without hurting her more," he said.

Without speaking, Na-to-si caught the rope and belayed it around a piñon. Then, as Uh-tatse pulled his wife up, yard by yard, his friend took up the slack and held her securely as he got a fresh grip.

Uhtatse hated to think what pain Ihyannah must be suffering. There would have been a child, he knew, in the spring. Now he feared terribly that there would not be a small one, perhaps ever. He had seen such things.

She made no sound as he pulled her over the lip of the cliff and caught her into his numbed arms. Na-to-si was running ahead of them to alert the old women, but the blood was still flowing, staining the snow and her skirt and his leggings.

"Ihyannah! Ihyannah!" he breathed into her ear. "Do not die! Only you make me into a man like my fellows. Without you I am a lonely wind, wandering the mesa. Live!"

A small chuckle came from the huddle in his arms. "Not so easily will you free yourself from me, Uhtatse." Then her body convulsed, and he ran still faster.

The old women were waiting beside the small hut set aside for births. Smoke rose from the smoke hole ... they must have brought fire from a cooking place.

Uhtatse held her out, and Kosiah, the midwife, took Ihyannah from him and carried her into the hut. The deer hide closed behind them.

Na-to-si touched his arm. "Come with me into my mother's house. Wait with us."

Uhtatse shook his head. He could not sit and wait. He had his work to do, even now.

"I will go out onto the mesa," he said. "If she ... if Ihyannah wants to see me, give the call. I will hear and I will come. I cannot ... I am grateful to you, but to sit with nothing to do but wait would drive me mad."

His friend nodded with understanding. Uhtatse turned away into the juniper wood and walked blindly for a long time. When he reached the edge of the cliff, he stopped and stood still to draw a deep breath.

The world settled again into its familiar pattern. He turned to do his work, pushing all the worry from his mind.

XIV

Uhtatse lay alone in Ihyannah's house, listening to the thin shriek of the wind among the stones. The pile of sleeping skins seemed chillier without Ihyannah's body curled against him. The night seemed blacker. While the isolation of the spot was just right for two, it was terrible for one alone.

It would be weeks before she could return to him. That was the prescribed time for purification after a birth or a miscarriage, and she must stay in the Women's House until that time had passed. There would be no small one in Ihyannah's house for a while.

Indeed, Kosiah had hinted that there might never be one. Sihala had wept, a thing he had never seen her do. When Uhtatse went to sit beside Ki-shi-o-te, waiting to know what happened, the old man was silent and sad, though it was not truly fitting for a man to worry so about a child of his own get. Only a sister's child should evoke such feeling.

Lying in the darkness, Uhtatse thought about the possibility that his wife might never have a child. He had been the youngest of Ahyallah's children, but he had lived closely with the others in the Big House. He had lived most of his life with the thin wails of babies in the night and the smell of the moss their mothers packed into their wrappings to catch the dung and urine.

It seemed a small thing to him, young as he was, that they would not have to suffer through the rearing of young ones. Then he thought of Lawi, Na-to-si's tiny sister. The two boys had known the joy of hearing her laughter. She clapped her small hands as they tossed her high or rode her about the mesa on their backs. That solid warmth of her small body had been a good thing.

A house would be very quiet if it never had little ones in it. This house, in particular, was entirely too quiet.

He turned to look toward the door-skin. The faintest light had begun to show around the edges. It was time, he was grateful to see, for him to go about his watching again.

His youngest sister had brought food sent by his mother, though she knew he could care for himself, as all the People could. He ate from the jar, the cold mess of beans and squash and corn almost frozen as he chewed. Then he donned all his winter gear and went again to climb the cliff and walk the mesa.

It occurred to him as he climbed to wonder how many years of this work would fall to his lot. The Old One had been active while men were born and lived and died. Would he survive to smell the wind for his people for an equally long span? But on this morning, he seemed not to care. Nothing seemed worthwhile.

He set his feet carefully, feeling the rope's reassurance. It would be easy, he thought, to chip toeholds in the cliff face. Yet that might make the descent too easy for any enemy who might try to reach the house. If, however, the notches were set just so—if one must begin the descent on the proper foot, for instance—then one who did not know would find himself in difficulties before he reached his goal.

Musing over this idea, he reached the top and looked about him. It was cold, but for once the wind had died away. Snow drifted down lazily, the flakes spaced widely. He almost felt warm, so great was the contrast with the chill brought by the wind.

He moved to the northern cliffs and stood there, staring over the white plain below the mesa. He opened all his senses, feeling afar, though he expected to sense nothing but the small stirrings of deer and other beasts forced from their lairs in search of food.

He smiled, his face stiff with chill. An eagle rode the wind, too far above for him to see, yet clear to his perceptions. A big cat prowled down in the Middle Way. He could feel the hunger rolling in its gut, the cold snow gritting beneath its paws.

He felt the start of terror in the deer it stalked. Very quickly thereafter came the darkness of death, and that was as it should be. The world was in balance, each kind sustaining others in a giant circle that was becoming clearer to him as he lived and performed his task.

That alone would have made his work worthwhile. Even Ki-shi-o-te, he found, had not learned all the perfection of the Circle, as he was doing. He honored his predecessor more every time he walked in his tracks, sinking more deeply into their mutual craft. The Old One had never intimated that he might know more of the world than his peers. He had never seemed arrogant, though now Uhtatse knew that he had a right to be.

He stiffened, all his senses focused on a point just below the mesa. There was life there. A human life, filled with weariness and fear. Near to the edge of death, if his sensing was not in error.

He searched minutely for other lives. Though the Kiyate had never been known to attack in winter, it was not impossible that they might. Yet there was no trace of any human spark except for the single one.

He felt rabbits in their burrows; birds huddled deep in the needled branches of piñons and junipers; snakes, chilly and inactive, in the dens they shared with gophers and prairie dogs. No other man-thing walked the plain, he knew for certain.

Uhtatse turned and sped toward his people's pueblo. As he passed those of other branches of the tribe, he called out, but he did not slack off his pace until he came to the Big House.

"One comes through the snow," he said to Ha-no-na-say, who had taken Ki-shi-o-te's place as Teacher. "He is alone, almost frozen, very weary and terribly afraid. Someone has pursued him, I think. Or something has. Perhaps one of the big cats thought to make a meal of him . . . and yet his fear seems more intense than such a matter would warrant."

There was no discussion. Six men put on their winter cloaks and their thick footgear and leggings and followed the One Who Smelled the Wind as he hurried along the mesa. Others from neighboring pueblos joined them along the way, and they at last began to descend the steep toward the pathway.

It was no easy journey. The path was now a trench filled with snow, and they had to tramp out a way to move through it. The distance was great, and they had to spend a night in a rock cleft, shivering in their cloaks, though they built a small fire of oak branches and deadfall.

They ate nothing, but that did not trouble them. They were used to going without food for long periods in winter. It made their stores last longer, and when they were inactive they used little energy. This effort was made on stored energy. Spring was still too far away to warrant the unnecessary consumption of food stores.

They packed close together, sharing their body heat. Uhtatse tried to sleep, but he could only wonder how it was with Ihyannah. He had managed to forget while he was moving through the snow. But now his mind busied itself again with his wife, and it was far into the night before he slept.

XV

As soon as first light touched the sky, revealing low-hanging clouds still pregnant with snow, they set out again, making directly for the point of warmth that Uhtatse could still feel. It flickered feebly now; the one in the snow would not last for long, and before he died they must learn if he brought any threat on his heels to the mesa of the Ahye-tum-datsehe.

He might himself be an enemy, freezing in the snow. They would leave him to his fate, if that were true. He was certainly a stranger, and the People seldom troubled themselves with strangers. Yet Uhtatse felt a compulsion when he first located the struggling life, and he felt it still. The one in the snow would not live to reach the mesa, and the One Who Smelled the Wind knew in his deepest sensing that that one bore some news of value to his own kind.

The wind rose after dawn and began blowing from the northeast. The light snow that had fallen just after daylight was turning into sleet as they plowed forward, following with blind faith where Uhtatse led.

As they rounded the last angle of the mesa's toes, the full blast caught them and tried to push them back the way they had come. Uhtatse motioned for the rest to shelter behind a tumble of boulders while he went forward.

"I will go," he shouted over the wind. "He is alone, near death. It is not far, and he can pose no threat to me. One man will frighten him less than all of us might do. Remain here, and I will return soon."

They obeyed, and he pushed onward against the thrust of the gale. That life was burning still, ahead of him, and he thought the man must have taken shelter among the rocks, even as his companions were doing. The weariness he felt in the man would prevent his going any closer to the bulk of the mesa.

Uhtatse did not call out. His language, he felt sure, would mean nothing to that other. And no shout could carry far into the teeth of that wind. He had to follow his sensing in order to find this stranger, whose life called out to him from such a distance.

He bumped against a tumble of boulders, blinded by the blown snow. Beyond that obstacle, he felt, he would find the one he sought. With numbed hands, he felt his way, moving around the pile and out of the worst of the wind. He could feel the man nearby now, within an arc of fallen rubble, which was half-roofed with a tilted slab of sandstone.

"Ohé," he said as quietly as he could over the noise of the wind. "Is someone here?"

There came a gasp from the darkness beneath the slab roof.

"*Kay hay na-te?*" The voice was so faint that it was almost drowned by the noise of the growing storm.

Uhtatse did not recognize the words. There was neither time nor light to use the sign language with which the Anensi had linked the tribes with whom they traded. He stooped and crawled beneath the shelter. Face-to-face with the other man, he stopped to look into the eyes gleaming at him from the dimness.

The man stared up from the huddle he had contrived from his own tattered deer-hide cloak and what looked like the remnant of a bearskin, like those the Anensi traded. A cold hand moved from beneath the pile and caught at Uhtatse's arm.

There was a clear question in the black eyes now, and Uhtatse made the sign for peace. Even in the gloom, the other recognized it and relaxed. There came a stirring as he unfolded himself from his garments and began crawling out to meet his rescuer.

This was a man of good sense, Uhtatse thought. There were many people, he suspected, who would have been too terrified to behave sensibly in these circumstances. It was not safe to go to the rescue of strangers. More than one of his kind had died at the hands of a man so frightened and warped by his fear that he did not recognize help and saw only threat.

He bent to help the man to his feet. Then he caught him about the waist, for he knew he was too weak to stand against the blast of the wind beyond the stones. And now that wind helped him, instead of pushing him back, as he moved from the shelter of the stones. It pushed at his back, hurrying him along his obliterated track toward the place where he had left the rest of his people.

The one he helped was struggling manfully to keep up without impeding him. Uhtatse understood the difficulty of making half-frozen limbs move and numbed feet take the weight imposed upon them. His respect rose with every yard the two of them traveled.

It was an effort to make their way back to the path, which had filled again with snow. Sleet had crusted over the top of that, and it was hard to break through to secure footing.

Yet the men who had come with Uhtatse persisted, and they gained the Middle Way by midafternoon. There still remained the terrible climb to the high mesa, and they felt they should wait for morning to attempt that. There were dwellings on the nearer side of this part of the mesa, and those who lived there, though not often visited, were their kindred. They would shelter the group for the night, though all agreed not to make any demands upon their store of food. There was a long winter still stretching ahead of them. They would eat when they returned to their own places.

They gained the first of the smaller houses on a gust of wind and sleet. Those inside welcomed a part of their number, but the house was too small for such a large group. Uhtatse spoke with the elders, made certain that the demands of politeness were met, and placed the man he had found in the care of the woman whose house this was. Then he forged onward, with the rest of his group, to find shelter in the large pueblo ahead.

Even as he drifted into sleep in a strange house, he wondered at himself. It had not been something he had thought deeply about as he performed the task, yet the decision to rescue that man in the snow had been extremely compelling. What secret did he know that was of value to the Ahye-tum-datsehe?

That question submerged his worry about Ihyannah, and that night Uhtatse fell asleep at once, as if someone had dashed his head against a rock.

△△△△△△△△△△△△△△△△△△△△△△△△△△△△△△△△△△△△△△△

XVI

▽▽▽▽▽▽▽▽▽▽▽▽▽▽▽▽▽▽▽▽▽▽▽▽▽▽▽▽▽▽▽▽▽▽▽▽▽

By the time the weary and famished men returned to their own pueblo, the storm had blown itself out, and only occasional snow flurries gusted across the mesa. The man they had brought with them had revived somewhat in the warmth of the house in the Middle Way, and during his stay the woman had insisted that he drink broth from her family's pot. That had given him some strength.

He was now less of a starved and beaten creature than he had been, more of a man than Uhtatse had yet seen him. He sat erect on the bench between Ki-shi-o-te and Ha-no-na-say, in the kiva. The other elders of the tribe were crowded into the space as well, and the small fire burning in the fire pit warmed the place well when aided by so many bodies.

Ha-no-na-say was the spokesman for the People, though he always consulted with Ki-shi-o-te before making pronouncements or asking questions. And the older Teacher had talked long with Uhtatse before he joined the group in the kiva. He knew the feelings of the One Who Smelled the Wind.

Ha-no-na-say tried questioning the newcomer, both in the tongue of the Ahye-tum-datsehe and that of the Anensi, but neither language was comprehensible to him. Even the sign language he used was slightly different from the one they had learned from the traders.

When he shook his head and made the sign for "far away," that did not astonish any of the people crowded into the room. His look and the remnant of his clothing told them that, as clearly as words could have done.

With signs, their guest told them of the raid that had struck his people in late summer. His entire camp had been burned, and the people either slaughtered or taken captive and driven away.

The faces of those listening were very grave as they watched the gestures that told them of the death of this man's woman and the captivity of his children. "Taken away into the north" was the ending gesture as from his tongue rolled a frightening name, while his hands returned to his sides.

"Tsununni."

That had not been a name unknown to them, though it had been a remote one. Still, it had been a name to fear, for those people scourged distant places and killed people they did not know. Now here was one who had suffered directly at their hands. It sent a chill of foreboding through every listener there.

Ha-no-na-say bowed his head to the speaker, who took his seat again. He turned to Ki-shi-o-te to ask, "And what was the word of the Old Woman Who Sings the Future?"

She was so old and wise, so highly respected, that it would almost have been thinkable to allow her to enter the kiva. Almost, but not quite, so her pronouncements must come from Ki-shi-o-te.

"She told me that she would go away into her own place to sing the future," he grunted. "Only for a small distance forward, and with the warning that the vision is not always easy to understand. There are matters that are not clear. She told me to wait, and she would return before the fire burned low in her fire basket."

The old man stared into the fire, and Uhtatse shifted slightly, impatient to hear what the old man would tell them. He thought of Ihyannah, for when things did not demand his immediate attention he always returned to thoughts of her.

How would he feel if his own woman had died at the hands of the Tsununni? His children taken away as slaves for the raiders . . . not all people were as peaceful or as secure as his own.

The Ahye-tum-datsehe took captive Kiyate from time to time, but they adopted them into the tribe. No one on the mesa was a slave of the kind the Anensi told them about in the lowland villages. Life was hard for all. There was work enough to weary every member of the People. Why should life be harder for one than another?

Ki-shi-o-te's voice jerked him from that thought. As he stared at his old friend, he realized that there was a dark color rising in the seamed cheeks. Uhtatse felt his heart thump as the old man gathered his strength to tell the Seeing of the Old Woman.

It had been a bad vision. Uhtatse could feel it, with the same senses he used in feeling out the beasts of the mesa. He could almost see a cold light rising in the room, chilling the hearts of all those who listened and watched.

The old man did not stand, for now not only his age but his terrible message had taken away his strength. When he spoke again, his voice was so weak that it almost was lost from time to time.

"These are the words of our Seer," he said. "Listen to them!" He drew a deep breath and began:

"I have sung the future, for a handful of years lying ahead of us. Beyond that there is no need to worry ourselves, not for a very long time." The old face assumed the very look of power that the Seer had when she told of things to come, and Uhtatse leaned forward to hear better.

"I have sung. The mesa stands, as it has done and as it will stand when we are no longer even memories here. Yet within a handful of seasons, we will be troubled by terrible things. I see winters harsher than any we have known. I see men fiercer than any Kiyate. I see blood on the stones. I see the People lying dead with their children and even the dogs and the parrots.

"Truly, this traveler has come on the edge of a long and terrible storm. The Tsununni will come to this place."

XVII

With those last forbidding words, the old man slumped, and Uhtatse leaned to catch him and ease him down. Ki-shi-o-te looked like one dead, his lined face waxy and his eye sockets rimmed with blue.

The One Who Smelled the Wind had seen the picture in the Old Woman's mind, even as the Shaman sang her vision. His sensitivity was so great now that he often found himself seeing impossible things through the eyes of people or creatures or even of their spirits. He had seen blood smeared on the golden sandstone outside the pueblo, painting it with bright color. The parrots lay with their necks wrung, tumbles of bright feathers lying beside those who had taken pleasure in them.

He squinched his eyes tightly, clasped his hands in his lap to stop their trembling. Then he rose from his crouch beside his friend. "I will take this man to the house of Ihyannah," he said, indicating the rescued traveler. "If that pleases him and my people, I will give him shelter. The pueblo is crowded in this ill weather, and there is room where I live."

Ha-no-na-say nodded. "Our sister Ihyannah will not object to such use of her house. That is well thought, Uhtatse. It is time we went to rest and to think. A time will come when there is no more opportunity for thinking. That will lend more value to what we do now."

The stranger, once he understood their meaning, came willingly behind Uhtatse to the edge of the cliff. When his host gestured toward the perilous way down, he stared with wonder and some hesitation. Uhtatse unrolled the cord and dropped it from the anchoring tree. The visitor looked relieved and came behind without pause as Uhtatse began the descent.

They found themselves on the ledge before the cave just as another spatter of snow mixed with sleet dashed against the face of the cliff. The shelter of the arched opening made the small house seem very warm as they entered it.

Uhtatse made fire, using the live coals that were preserved in a heavy pot filled with charcoal for such purposes. He set the big jar of fermented corn to warm and sliced meat from a haunch of a deer that Ihyannah had hung in a far corner of the cave to keep in the freezing weather.

All the while they ate, he was wondering how he might convey to the man his need to have him relive the thing that had sent him fleeing toward the mesa. He knew he could read the pictures formed in the stranger's mind if he would only recall the events from beginning to end in an orderly way.

Yet how could he tell this alien person what he wanted him to do? He bent his head over the jar, digging out gobbets of the thick stuff with his fingers. As he chewed, the other man reached to touch his hand.

"Karenni," he said, pulling Uhtatse's fingers to touch his own chest.

"Uhtatse."

"Ooh-tat-see?" Karenni asked. Then, in a moment, "Uhtatse." He nodded with satisfaction.

Uhtatse nodded, too, and smiled. It was obvious that the man wanted to communicate, if they could manage a way to do it.

He thought of all the sign language he had learned over the years and made a gesture for sleep. But he qualified that with the one for dreaming, as well. He indicated a hunter reading sign while tracking game. It might be a terrible jumble, but the stranger seemed to be following what he was doing.

Uhtatse touched his own forehead, squinted his eyes to show that he saw far. Then he touched Karenni's forehead and stared as if seeing into the man's mind. He had never tried to communicate such thoughts before. He wondered if his intention was clear at all, yet

Karenni nodded again. His motion was decisive, as if he had come to some sort of conclusion.

He motioned toward the pile of skins in the corner. Then he closed his eyes and pantomimed laying his head back for sleep. He opened his eyes again and stared intently at Uhtatse.

"I think you understand," breathed the One Who Smelled the Wind. "We will try."

He banked the fire carefully in the pit, taking out coals for the pot and filling the rest of the container with twigs and charcoal to keep them alive. Then he moved in the darkness to his own sleeping skin. He spread it beside that of Karenni and lay back, relaxing as much as he could manage to do.

His mind reached out, as it did on the mesa when he checked on the welfare of the deer. He found the warm spark that was his companion. He concentrated, as he had done while seeing the pictures from the mind of the Old Woman. There was a moment of confusion, as he saw something he could not quite identify.

He stood . . . among trees? Yet he had never seen trees so large. These towered above him, and he could hear wind humming in their branches so high overhead that they were only a dim mass. He felt the wind now, cool and clean as the air of the mesa, yet tanged with a scent that was not the familiar odor of juniper and piñon. A fresh smell, mixed with others that he knew were earth scents, though very unlike those he knew.

He became conscious of a weight against his back. A small deer, came the thought. So. He had been hunting. He was going home, for the forest was dim with approaching night.

He went quickly through that alien wood, slipping silently through undergrowth and between tree trunks that were many times the girth of his body. Then he paused. He had heard a cry in the distance.

He hung the carcass in a tree and set out at a lope for the source of that sound. The forest was growing darker, but the sky above the distant crests was still bright with sunset light. He scrambled over outcrops of stone that thrust themselves up from the forest floor, but still he hurried onward.

Uhtatse could feel a tight knot of apprehension in his throat and knew that he was feeling what Karenni had felt as he hurried toward his family. He burst from the wood into a small clearing, but he did not pause. Three men lay dead amid the grass, all men he knew. But they were gone, and he could not help them.

Into the wood he plunged again, running hard now. Those lance shafts had been decorated with scarlet and black feathers, and that meant Tsununni.

The sun was below the horizon when he came into a larger clearing, where the skin houses his tribe used in summer, while moving after the game, were set about haphazardly along the meandering stream cutting through the center of the rough circle. The houses were collapsing, burning. Bodies lay on the ground.

He flew to the one that had been his woman's. As he came, she crawled from beneath the flaming poles and blackened skins. Her hair was smoldering, and her deer-hide tunic was covered with blood. She was moving, but barely.

He bent to help her, to beat out the fire in her hair and her clothing. He pulled her to the creek and washed her face and dashed water on the sparks.

There was an arrow in her chest. Every time he looked at it, something inside him quivered with pain and rage. That was a wound that always proved fatal, and blood was already coming from the corner of her mouth.

Her eyes opened, staring up at him, as if pleading or commanding. Uhtatse, caught in that other memory, did not truly understand her words, but he had Karenni's own knowledge of their meaning.

"The children!" she choked. She gasped and forced her failing tongue to move again. "Tsununni. Took. Children. East."

Her life was leaving her, even as she spoke. Only such a will as hers could have kept her alive for long enough to give her message. As her eyes glazed and her body went limp with the laxity of death, Karenni lifted her in his arms and turned back toward her skin house.

It was blazing fiercely. He laid her beneath the leaning edge and pulled the thing over her with a pole that he retrieved from the creek bank.

As he stood beside the fire that took her, his heart was filled with agony. She was gone. And she had laid upon him her last concern and command.

The children! The children! The children!

XVIII

Uhtatse gazed up into the blackness of the room. Karenni had withdrawn into a flood of pain so terrible that it was anguish to touch his mind. He reached across the space between their sleeping skins to touch the man's shoulder. Surely a warm hand in the darkness might comfort him, no matter how little.

He heard the man draw a sharp breath. Then Karenni sighed, and with the sound of that in his ears, Uhtatse slept.

When he awoke, the room was filled with the tiny slivers of light that could make a way into the cavern and through the edges of the hide door. Its brightness hinted at sunlight ... the storm must have ended.

Uhtatse sat and turned to look at his guest, a huddled mass in the dimness. Karenni was gazing back at him, the soft glimmer of his eyes speculative. This was, he felt certain, a very wise man.

It would have been almost impossible to explain even to his own people, using their common tongue, the thing he had attempted the night before. Yet Karenni had grasped the concept without words, intuitively. Could he have been, among his own kind, one with the sort of sensing that Uhtatse possessed? This was impossible to learn until they shared a language.

He rose and rolled away his sleeping skins. Then he reached into the rapidly diminishing jar of corn, which he had set in the firepit on top of the warm ash to keep its contents from freezing overnight.

Karenni came to squat beside him and ate hungrily from the congealed mass. Too soon, the bottom of the jar came into view. Uhtatse shrugged and grimaced. He must cook more food, now, which was a thing he had been glad to turn over to Ihyannah.

Karenni smiled. Then he glanced inquiringly at his host, obviously wondering if Uhtatse spent all his days alone in this isolated house, instead of sitting with the men in the kiva, talking and working and playing games.

Uhtatse knew it would be very difficult to explain to him the work of the One Who Smells the Wind, even if they went onto the mesa together so that Karenni could observe him at his task. But he decided to try it.

Gesturing toward the pile of skins and furs, he indicated that Karenni was to find a pelt to use for a cloak. Then Uhtatse wrapped himself well and moved out onto the shelf of rock at the lip of the ledge.

For the first time in days, the sun showed through the cloud cover. The warm light was turning the cliffs across the canyon to gold, as the two men turned to climb the difficult stair to the top of the mesa. As Uhtatse's head rose over the top of the cliff, he looked up into the piñon leaning above him. Every needle was outlined in light as the sunlight caught in the ice that encrusted it.

The scents of pine and juniper were sharp in the cold wind. A hawk sat in a juniper at a little distance, and Uhtatse could feel it ruffle its feathers to shut out the wind, snap its beak irritably, and work its muscles in preparation for its morning hunt.

A sense of the wonder of this world and its creatures overcame him, as it often did. This time it was touched with a pang of sadness . . . how easily his people might lose this life, for it was never secure, even at its best. Now there was an edge of danger, like a storm cloud, on the fringes of all his perceptions.

He stood and helped Karenni up the last of the way. Then he coiled his cord neatly and hung it in the anchor tree. Only then did he turn to his companion.

He laid his fingers across his eyes. Then he swept his hand in a circle, indicating the entire mesa, the air above it and the plain below. He touched his ears. Again his hands swept in a circle. He put a finger to his nose, inhaling mightily. As if he had scented something strange and important, he nodded and stared about him.

With sudden clarity, he knew that Karenni was putting all of this together and was understanding that it was not only by chance that he had been rescued from the storm. His eyes widened, and he laid a cold hand on Uhtatse's shoulder. When Uhtatse moved upwind toward the northwest quarter of the mesa, Karenni was at his heels.

In no way did he vary his way of working across the land. But at every step he felt the newcomer studying him and the mesa, the creatures that had ventured from nests and burrows, and the way in which Uhtatse stood as he sensed every quarter of his domain.

Today, knowing that somewhere beyond the horizon the Tsununni must be planning their spring raids, he concentrated even more strongly. He sent his perceptions to the limits of their capacity. He did not expect any enemy to be near, even on the lowlands, for no one made war in winter. This very harsh winter was even less likely than most to harbor those who intended immediate raids. Yet the act of trying seemed to relieve his worry a bit.

Though the mesa was a difficult climb, it was not too difficult for those who intended to attack. Only the sheer cliffs facing upon the interior canyons were impassable, except for single climbers in a few locations. The slopes toward the lower lands were less forbidding. Many men could go quickly to the Middle Way. From there they could make their way upward in any of a dozen directions.

Watchers for so many places could not be spared in the summer. Farming and hunting, making cord and pots, tending the catchments, all those required many hands. A hundred different tasks made survival over the winter possible for the Ahye-tum-datsehe. So in summer he would be the one who would stand, with only a few watchers, between his people and invasion by the pitiless Tsununni.

He could remember one attack by the Kiyate. Now, recalling it, he thought that it had been more like a very serious game, to which both the Ahye-tum-datsehe and the Kiyate knew all the rules. He had been a child, and Ahyallah had put him, with his sisters, in a room deep inside the pueblo. That room was crammed with children, and he remembered the thick smell of their bodies and the feeling of tension in the air.

His mother had taken her light bow, her basket of arrows, and the heavy stick with a burl at one end and gone to stand guard at the entrance door of the pueblo, with the other young women. Stretched along the ground by the wall or hidden in rooms inside, waiting to take the place of any who were killed, were many people, old and young.

Even the oldest of them were armed, stationed in rooms near the entrance. Before the Kiyate could come to the place where the children were hidden, they would have to kill almost every woman of the Ahye-tum-datsehe.

He had seen nothing of the fighting, of course. When the noise of the conflict was over, the Kiyate driven back down the steeps, he had stood, wide eyed, in a circle of children. He had watched the wounded as they were plastered with healing mud or had their gaping wounds stitched together with bone needles and yucca fiber.

Now he understood what the men had been saying while they ignored the pain of their injuries: "What fools, the Kiyate, to begin their attack with the bird-off-the-nest!" He could still hear the words of Ki-shi-o-te. He knew now that the term meant a noisy feint meant to draw the defenders from their positions, making it easy for a large body of men to breach the defenses of the Big House.

He drew himself from the memory and stood on the cliff edge, looking over the plain. It now shone unbearably bright with sunlight on snow.

That had been a game in which every move was known and understood. Each strategy had a name and was recognizable almost at once to both sides for what it was.

It had been a long time before he had the chance to ask Ki-shi-o-te what the Kiyate might hope to gain from their attacks on the mesa villages. He could still hear the old man's reply.

"They wander, the Kiyate, from place to place, never stopping to grow crops, only gathering the wild seeds that grow on the plains. They want our stores of corn and beans and squash to help them live through the winter. Some years they go in one direction, some in another. They find it easier, I suspect, in places unprotected by the mesa and our stout houses of stone. We seldom see them."

"But if they never get anything, why do they keep coming?" he asked, puzzled.

"Oh, they always go away with something. They send scroungers to hunt out our storage places in the sides of the cliffs. We cannot spare the warriors to defend those and the pueblos, as well. They have, in the past, overcome pueblos on other parts of the mesa and taken their stores. If attacking us did them no good, you can be certain that they would not come."

It still seemed strange to Uhtatse that those people had not learned to settle in one spot and attend to their own wants. However, every kind had its own ways, as he was learning from the things Ra-onto had told him.

Now he knew that his own people probably would one day face an enemy whose tactics they did not know and could not hope to decipher quickly enough to make an adequate defense. The thought frightened him.

It occurred to him that the pueblos were not as easily defended as he had thought. They had many outer doors, warrens of rooms, all opening into each other. An enemy attacking with fire would probably set the roof stringers of juniper ablaze and bring the whole structure down onto the heads of those inside it. Young ones in their middle rooms could not get out through smoke and battle. They would be frightened, too, and confused if that should happen. And with a totally ruthless enemy, it could very possibly happen.

The Kiyate had wanted stores, and they did not want to burn them. But the Tsununni ... what did they want? They had taken Karenni's children as slaves. Perhaps they would want the People for slaves as well, driving them from their defenses with fire.

There had to be a better way to defend the Ahye-tum-datsehe. He wished that he knew where it was that Karenni had last seen sign of the Tsununni. How long would it take for them to find the mesa and to see that a prosperous people lived on its top?

As if reading his thought, Karenni came to stand beside Uhtatse. He stared away across the plain toward the northeast. Then he squatted on the snowy cliff edge and broke a twig from a juniper beside him. Smoothing a patch of snow, he drew a stick figure man holding a lance in a threatening attitude.

He glanced up to make certain that Uhtatse

was following his motions. Then he drew again. Uhtatse decided that he was giving an account of flatlands and streams and arroyos and other mesas. He even used his hand to shape the snow into hillocks and gashes. At the very edge of the drawing, he made a tall ridge of snow, gapped with many peaks.

Uhtatse knew that east of the mesa stood mountains. His own people had visited there a few times. He said the word for mountain and made jagged motions in the air, indicating the peaks, to make sure that was what Karenni meant.

The man nodded. His finger pointed beyond those jagged heights and then to himself. In his own turn, Uhtatse nodded. He had traveled very far, indeed, over country that must have been harsh for one traveling alone and without supplies.

Now Karenni was making long marks in the snow. Beside each, he set the prints of his five fingers. That brought him to the edge of the first flat space, probably plain or desert. That was still very far, and at least a season of travel for a single man.

It took some time for Karenni to complete the sketch of his journey. Uhtatse thought he must have been on his way for at least eight or ten moons. When the pattern was outlined in the snow, with the time spans for each part, Karenni touched his shoulder and pointed urgently toward a spot in a lower range of mountains that he had mounded between two wide flat spaces.

"Tsununni!" he said urgently. "Tsununni!"

Uhtatse counted the time marks between that spot and the lump that he thought was the mesa. The better part of a year. Then he thought of the man's children. If he had found the Tsununni, why had he not freed them or died in the attempt?

He turned from the pattern and smoothed another patch of snow. On it he drew small rounded shapes, three, which was the number he had felt in the words of the dying woman. Beside those he drew a stick man and then pointed to Karenni.

He made the gesture that indicated a question.

Karenni sank onto his heels and stared away over the plain. His expression was impassive, as it usually was, but in his eyes there was pain. After a moment, he stretched his hand toward the crude drawing.

With infinite care, he rubbed away the three small drawings, leaving the stick man alone on the expanse of snow. Uhtatse looked away, knowing that his expression would reveal his understanding and his pain. He was still too young to mask his feelings as this man did.

They stood together and went forward again, quartering the mesa. Neither spoke nor tried to communicate again.

Uhtatse's mind was busy with the problem

his people must face sooner or later. How could he help them protect themselves when the Tsununni came?

Suddenly, into his mind came a picture that had formed there when Ra-onto told him of the cities in the south. Tall cliffs of houses. Tall cliffs. Unscalable cliffs, for any warlike purposes.

His own house sat snugly in its cranny, and one man could hold off hundreds at need.

His step lightened. He felt his heart give a great surge of warmth, like triumph. If he could persuade his people to try it, that might save all their lives in the years to come.

XIX

Uhtatse brought Ihyannah home from the Women's House to her own home at last, though he had to wait until he could find a span of clear weather to do it. She was not disturbed, he found, to share her space with their guest. The thing that bothered her was the lack of cooked food and the clutter of debris that the men had allowed to accumulate.

When Uhtatse told her how the man had come to them, as well as the way which he had lost his family, she went out of her way to make Karenni welcome. Ihyannah felt even for a fallen birdling or a crushed insect. A man so injured by circumstance brought out all her best instincts. She undertook at once to teach Karenni the language of the Ahye-tum-dat-sehe, knowing that Uhtatse could not spare so much time. He did, however, contribute what he could.

It was as well that he did, for blizzard followed blizzard until the snow was so deep that he gave up his travels upon the mesa until the weather became warmer. No enemy of any sort could move in such conditions, and it was foolish to risk his life and his bones to the deep snow, the icy wind, and the slick rock faces.

The pair had stored their grain and jerked venison and hare, their dried squash and beans and piñon nuts in a deep cleft at the back of the cave in which their house was set. This attracted mice, which also added fresh meat to their diet. They were well supplied with food, and for water they had only to fill a jar with snow and set it near the coals that they kept smoldering in their fire pit, feeding them from the supply of dried branches that Ihyannah had let down the cliff face all summer, when she found the time.

One day when the wind howled even into the cave, rippling the door-skin against its ties and flapping it on the cut stone of the walls, the three were sitting close to the pit, wrapped in their sleeping skins. Uhtatse, who had been thinking hard about an idea since it had come to him on the mesa, began telling them about the houses that could be built, as theirs had been, into the sides of the cliffs.

"There are hundreds of caves, some very large . . . big enough for true pueblos . . . some sized for several houses, and some so small that only one dwelling could fit into them. If our people would build in those, taking their

families and their dogs and parrots down into
the caves, no attacker could ever come against
us in our houses. They might damage crops in
the fields above, but they could not reach the
supplies in the caves or the people protected in
such places.

"Think of it . . . I could stand at the foot of our
path with a club or a spear and hold off a hundred of the Kiyate or the Tsununni. Ihyannah
could as well, or even a child, if he were large
enough. The hold on the cliff, without the cord,
which would be brought down every time the
last person came from above, is so fragile that
any pressure could pry a climber loose to fall
into the canyon. There could be no safer place."

"And if winters are harsh like this one in
times to come, the people would be much
warmer here than up there in the full blast of
the wind," added Ihyannah.

Karenni, who had learned very quickly with
both of them teaching him, leaned forward, following the conversation. He nodded, though it
took him a moment to find the words he
wanted.

"If my own people could have been protected
so, they would be alive now. Not dead," he said.

They shivered; their faces, red lit by the
coals, were turned toward Uhtatse now. He
could see in their eyes that they found his notion promising.

"We know the mesa as nobody else can do,"
he went on. "We can, if we want to, attack the

invaders from spots they cannot know to exist. We could, in an emergency, even . . . set fire to the juniper."

At Ihyannah's gasp of protest, he shook his head. "I understand your feeling. Such a move would condemn me to all the small deaths it would cause. Only if there was a terrible need, and only if the wind was right, so that the fire would not spread where we did not want it, could we do such a thing. But it is a possibility."

Karenni was sitting upright, his covering slipped aside, unnoticed. His eyes were very bright.

"This . . . could save your people . . . from the fate that my own people suffered," he said.

Ihyannah's eyes narrowed as she thought out the plan. "You must take this thought to Ha-no-na-say and the Healer and the Old Woman, as well as the Speaker for the Women. It is unusual. Never before, I think, has anyone had such a thought. As you say, it is only for the most desperate time we can imagine, but it is not to be forgotten because of that."

"When the wind dies, the snow is not so deep, and the way up the cliff becomes possible, I will take this thought to the Council," said Uhtatse. "I did not want to speak until I had smoothed away any problems I could find in it. And there is still one that I could not smooth away . . . it will be terrible labor. Think how difficult it was to build this tiny house. How heavy the stones were! How weary we all became before the thing was done! Few will be happy at the thought of such work."

His wife's eyes glittered in the reddish light. "If all the Ahye-tum-datsehe work together, it will not be too hard. We can twist ropes, along with our cords, all through the winters. In the spring we can begin cutting sandstone blocks, while those who do not can work harder than usual at growing the crops and hunting the game and gathering the yucca and juniper bark and the wild plants and herbs. It can be done.

"The time will come when only such a decision can save us from the thing that happened to Karenni's people. I feel that to be true, even I who am not the One Who Smells the Wind. Do you not feel it, Uhtatse?"

Without speaking, he nodded. He had been feeling it for weeks now.

She smiled sadly. "We have no child, but others do. We must save them, must make certain that our people do not die at the hands of the Tsununni or go away with them as slaves. Karenni has come to us, seemingly by chance, but how strange it is that his coming will be likely to save our people. The gods work strangely, and the god of snow and storm sent him straight to our door."

It was not the first time Uhtatse had thought of that. "You will argue the notion with your father?" he asked her. "He will listen to you even more readily than to me. I will take it to Ha-no-na-say and the other Elders." A thought occurred to him, and he sighed. "The women will not like leaving their homes."

"They will go to better ones," snapped Ihyan-nah. "I will bring all who will come down here to my house, and they can see how warm we are, while they are shivering over their tiny braziers and coughing in the smoke of their pueblo. The men spend their days in the kivas and do not suffer so, but it is uncomfortable in the Big House in winter. The wind comes in without taking the smoke away with it. Here, our smoke can go out into the air, and we can build as big a fire as we want, though we do not need a big one because of the shelter of the stone."

Uhtatse grinned at her. "Then your task will be to persuade the women. No man could hope to do that. My mother, I think, will see the sense in such a move and may help you. And the Old Woman . . . she is strange. She saw her Vision, and I think that she will agree with us."

The girl nodded, staring into the fire. Uh-tatse put his arm about her and stared too, seeing in the dancing flickers the long task that his people might face if they adopted his plan.

XX

It seemed, as they sat beside their fire and made their plans, to be a thing that might be simple to decide, though it might be difficult to do. Now, dreaming in the cold wind, old Uhtatse knew that they had been terribly young and very inexperienced in the ways of people.

It seemed forever since he could have been so young, so ignorant of the tendency of mankind to do as he has done, rather than trying something new. He had gone to Ha-no-na-say, filled with the strength of his conviction, only to find that what the young propose the old usually oppose on principle.

Even Ki-shi-o-te, understanding both the danger from increasingly severe winters and the threat of the Tsununni, objected to the notion of living underground like a prairie dog or a mole. "I have lived my life like a man, standing upon the mesa and facing the wind," he said to Ihyannah, and not even his favorite could persuade him.

Ha-no-na-say said nothing, but his eyes narrowed, and his thin nose seemed to become even thinner as he listened. He did not make any comment other than, "I will talk it over with the Elders. I will consult with the Old Woman Who Sings the Future, as well as the Speaker for the Women. Then I will give you an answer."

When Uhtatse returned for his reply, he shook his grizzled head. "We do not want to live differently. We do not have the time or the strength to build new houses, and to build them in such difficult places would double the work. No, Uhtatse. You are the One Who Smells the Wind. When you smell the enemy on the wind, then come again to me with your words."

It was shortsighted and stupid, but he had not known then that people tended to be shortsighted and stupid until the time of peril was upon them. Matters were not desperate, thought the Ahye-tum-datsehe. They had not seen, as he had, the death of Karenni's wife and the devastated skin houses.

One refugee from beyond the mountains did not mean surely that the Tsununni would come to the mesa at all, and if they did it would not be soon. The pueblos were big and comfortable and full of life. Why take upon themselves terrible labors and dangerous efforts that might be for nothing?

Nothing that Uhtatse could say persuaded them. He was, after all, a man of only sixteen summers, and they were elders who had lived for many hands of years. He could not sway them.

With the women, Ihyannah had a bit better luck. They liked the snug small house in the cliff, though they looked with suspicion at the long drop over which their children might fall and the perilous steep up which they had to climb. In the end, they elected to stay in their familiar houses, for the pueblos belonged to them, as did the fields. They hated to turn their backs upon them.

Only the One Who Sang the Future stood with them when the final decision was made. "I have seen much," she said. "I do not always understand the things that come to me as I sing, but it seems that there are dreadful times to come on this mesa. Times that will teach us the value of new ways of thinking and of living.

"We will look back upon this day, it may well be, with bitter grief, and we will sing laments over parents and children, men and women, and claw our breasts and toss ashes into our hair, but it will be too late."

She looked about at the group of elders, who stood on the roof of the kiva in the chill wind. "People do not like change. I do not like change, for I am old and my body aches and I dream ill dreams. Yet I say that this is a good thing that the One Who Smells the Wind proposes.

Strange days lie ahead. It is better to meet them from a place of strength than one of weakness."

She folded her arms over her flat chest, holding her winter robe tightly about her shrunken body. She stepped backward into a group of women and stared contemptuously about her, knowing that these people would not do what was wise, no matter what she said. When had they ever done so?

A shiver moved through the others standing there. Uhtatse could see it ripple along their ranks like breeze through aspen leaves. Ha-no-na-say turned to Ki-shi-o-te, and the two muttered softly together. The Healer for Women leaned to consult with the Healer for Men.

For some time, there was quiet conversation again among those who held the future of the People in their hands. At last, Ha-no-na-say stepped forward.

"We have thought even longer, after hearing this proposal. We have heard the words of our sister who sings the future. We have listened to the One Who Smells the Wind. We know their hearts to be sound, and we understand that they believe truly what they say. Yet we cannot agree.

"There is no danger here, and there never has been one on our mesa that we could not resist and conquer. Harsh winters, raids of the Kiyate, plagues of sickness, all those have come and gone, and still the People endure."

There was a murmur of agreement, and Uhtatse felt his heart sink again. The words of the Old Woman had not swayed them.

"To undertake such efforts, merely on the chance that danger may come in the future, would be a foolish thing. We would neglect our hunting, our farming, all the things that make life possible here. Our lives are not easy, at best. With such a project undertaken, they would become much harder. So we say no. We will not go, like moles, under the ground. We will not shelter, like swallows, in the crevices of the cliffs. Let any who wish to follow Uhtatse and Ihyannah build houses in the cliff faces, with the help of their own families. The People cannot spare the time for it."

Uhtatse felt Ihyannah's presence just behind him. He knew that she would have taken his hand in hers, if that had not been unseemly. He heard her whisper, barely audible, drift to his ear.

"We have begun it. Others will do as we have done, to get away from the noise of the pueblos. But what will become of the rest, when the Tsununni come?"

There was despair in her voice. It matched that in his heart.

XXI

As soon as the worst of the snow melted, Uh-tatse began finding his sister Umeya visiting Ihyannah, though the two had not been close friends before. He thought for a time that his mother was sending her to help Ihyannah with her work, until she was fully strong again. And then he noticed that she was talking far more with Karenni than with her sister-in-law.

He was not surprised when, in the early spring, Karenni approached him somewhat timidly. "Umeya has asked me to share her quarters in the pueblo," he said bluntly. "She is a strong woman, very good and bright, and I am lonely for a wife. I will go, if you do not mind. It is time that I leave you and your own woman alone together again."

Uhtatse smiled. "I have not had a brother," he said. "And it is important to respect the one who will be the father of my sister's children. I could not choose a better mate for Umeya than my friend Karenni."

For a few weeks he and Ihyannah reveled in being alone again, but as spring warmed and the time came for clearing the gardens and readying them for planting, they decided to move onto the mesa again, living in a pit house that was no longer used, now that the family had taken a new room in the Big House.

This allowed Ihyannah more hours in which to work in her plantings, and it also let Uhtatse range the mesa more closely. In spring, things tended to happen. The animals were restless—indeed, he felt the same restlessness humming along his own bones and through his nerves.

As well, the weather turned fickle, lashing the mesa with storms of lightning and wind, though little rain fell.

The Kiyate had been known to attack in spring, though; if their purpose was to seize winter foodstuff, Uhtatse could not understand why that should be so. They would not need such supplies for months, and those on the mesa were depleted almost completely. Perhaps, he thought, it was their nature to attack what lay in their way as they wandered over the plains in their obscure patterns, along their familiar routes.

Many nights he slept out on the mesa, his body in a light doze and all his senses alert. The warning brought by Karenni seemed to have honed him to a fine edge, all his nerves recording his sensings, interpreting them, discarding those that did not pose a threat.

As spring moved toward early summer, he saw Ihyannah less and less frequently. She came from the gardens weary, and when he came home from watching the mesa he was exhausted as well. They would smile at each other over the flames in the fire pit, and he would pour an offering down the *sipapu*. Then they would sleep, cuddled together like children, taking comfort from their closeness.

It was as well that Uhtatse was young. If he had been old, the harsh requirements he imposed upon himself might well have made him ill. He was still, however, little more than a boy. Seventeen winters tallied his age, and he was tough as juniper root and flexible as grass. The chill of the spring mornings did not bother him, though he dressed himself only in a g-string and sandals. The sun-drenched days of watching and the nights of prowling about the mesa did not trouble him at all.

He did not allow his thought of the Tsununni to distract his attention from matters nearer and more pressing. He felt the weather as pressures changed and humidities rose and fell. He foretold two storms, both severe, in time for the people to gather wild crops that were near their time and would have been ruined by the wind and hard rain.

That, more than anything, impressed his people. They had all been safely in the pueblo or the pit houses when the terrific lightnings and thunders rolled over the mesa, followed by winds that bent the junipers and piñons flat and flung before them the unusually heavy and stinging drops wrung from the clouds.

That rain washed out some of the catchments, damaging the systems of channels and small dams, but without warning the damage might have been much worse. Uhtatse had helped to carry stones to strengthen the waterways, and those so reinforced held against the storm.

Not a single one of his people was lost, though word came from other parts of the mesa that members of other tribes had been struck by the storm gods, dying in their fields on down in the Middle Way while harvesting roots and plants. This caused his reputation to grow, although still Ha-no-na-say would not listen to any word he spoke about moving the People into the cliffsides.

Still, he stopped to talk with the elders from time to time, trying to persuade them to consider his proposal. He felt that if he continued to press for the change, by the time he was an elder himself, he might have made some progress.

Going home one evening for a long-delayed reunion with his wife, he found Ihyannah sitting outside the pit house, chewing on a bit of venison. She rose at once when he came and brought food for him. She worried because for days at a time he lived upon whatever he found where he walked over the rough terrain. Insects, to her way of thinking, were unfit for human consumption unless starvation was at hand.

She brought a flat meal cake and a large piece of jerky. He dropped onto the ground beside her in the shadow of the line of junipers standing between their position and the edge of the cliff.

The sun was almost down, and they watched the sky go red and then orange. It was a thing they loved to see, although the reason was not one they could put into words.

Uhtatse waited until the sky went gray with twilight to eat. Then he finished and took Ihyannah's hand. For once, neither was too weary for love, and they went into their house and gave and took pleasure until they fell asleep.

The summer came. Plantings were growing, and it became clear that once again Ihyannah was with child. It did not slow her work in the fields or her evening tasks of twisting fiber or making baskets. Yet Uhtatse, coming more often to her house now to check on her welfare, saw with concern that she was pale, and dark shadows outlined her eyes.

He could not in decency discuss that with anyone, even his mother. The nearest he could come was to ask her, "Is all well with Ihyannah?"

Ahyallah smiled, but he could see concern to match his own in her eyes. "I cannot tell that anything is wrong," she told him.

Her words did not comfort him.

By midsummer, he had relaxed a bit. Seldom did anything perilous occur when the sun was beating on the plain below like a great fist, pounding the moisture out of the soil and drying up the few and scanty streams. Travel was almost as difficult then as in winter, for water was very hard to find and none of the Kiyate had ever come at such a time.

Storms were infrequent and he could smell them long before any cloud could be seen from the mesa. Animals stayed close to their drinking places, and even predators were not active. So he stayed near Ihyannah, doing the things that he could to help her, those that would not damage his gift. He could not pick beans or squash, for instance, but he could carry the laden baskets to the stone where Ihyannah dried them.

He saved her every step he could, but still she became paler and thinner, her child thrusting itself out before her in a lump. Her motions became slow, almost painful. As the time passed, he felt her weakness, and it dismayed him. Other women even nearer their time were awkward and tired, but they did not seem as ill as Ihyannah did.

He was not surprised when she cried out one night, calling for her mother. He carried her to

the Women's House even before he went for
Sihala. Kosiah, as if sensing the need for her
services, was coming from the pueblo, coughing
in the cool night air.

Uhtatse knew there was no point in staying
near the Women's House. He would be told
nothing, for the women considered such matters entirely their own business and no concern
of any man. So he went away in the darkness,
moving across the mesa.

He could feel her pain and fear, just as he did
those of the animals and birds and reptiles of
the mesa. A natural birthing, he'd found, con-
veyed no pangs to him. He had learned to
screen his mind from the normal pains of his
kind. But Ihyannah was too close to him. Her
suffering was his own.

He staggered through the junipers, his body
beaded with cold sweat. Could she live through
something so terrible? At last he turned toward
Sihala's house, knowing that Ki-shi-o-te was
also shut away from his favorite. He would be
worrying, no matter how he disguised the fact.

He found the old man sitting outside in the
starlight. He looked like some gnarled juniper
root, cross-legged in the darkness. He looked up
as Uhtatse came near. His hand came up in a
silent greeting, but neither of them spoke.

Uhtatse sat on the ground beside the old man
and stared away into the darkness. The stars
moved overhead, and a rag of moon rose at last
to cast reddish light over the mesa.

Like blood, Uhtatse thought.

As if hearing the thought, Ki-shi-o-te spoke at last. "There will be no child this time. It is a bad beginning. I have seen it often ... some have this happen again and again, until the woman dies of it. Few who begin so ever live to bear a child that lives."

Uhtatse felt his heart chill inside him. Was his Ihyannah doomed to that fate? Was he doomed to share her torture every year for as long as she lived? That was terrible to think about. He closed his eyes, trying to shut the rending and pulsing of her pain away from his perceptions.

Suddenly, it eased. He gasped and sat upright.

Ki-shi-o-te leaned to grasp his arm. "What have you felt? Tell me! It is improper, but I suffer for my child!"

Uhtatse drew a deep breath. Then he said, "It has stopped. She is delivered or she is dead. I cannot tell which."

Again the silence descended, and this time it was touched with a hint of doom. The moon rode up the sky overhead. Pale light touched the east.

Sihala came with first light, dragging her weary feet up the track from the Women's House. She looked at the two sitting outside her house with disapproving eyes, but she said nothing, knowing that people did not always behave in socially approved ways.

"She lives," the old woman said. "The child is dead. If you could call it a child. It was far too soon. Go to sleep, both of you. There is nothing that anyone can do now. She will live or she will die, and in time we will know which it will be."

When she turned away, there was no sound.

Uhtatse, however, felt her deep sorrow, and he knew that she was weeping.

XXII

Ihyannah lived. That one spark of warmth comforted Uhtatse as he worried about his responsibilities to the Ahye-tum-datsehe. Winters followed summers, springs followed winters, and still she lived, though she did not ever carry a child to term.

He began spending time, in the worst weather, in the kivas with men of the different tribes on the mesa. There was time, when the snow blew, to argue at length and for those with whom he spoke to think hard about his words. Though Ha-no-na-say and the elders still held firm, he kept trying to persuade the people of the joined mesas to think about moving their dwellings down into the cliffs.

Some visited Ihyannah's house in the winter and agreed that it afforded unusual comfort when the winds blew cold. Yet no other followed their example, even when it became obvious that they would not return to the pueblo, though there was now room for them.

Karenni and Umeya, in time, produced a son and two daughters, and Uhtatse devoted much time, as was the custom, to his sister's children. That, to some extent, soothed his grief over Ihyannah's repeated miscarriages. She, however, had no such comfort.

She worked hard all year, but in spring and summer she seemed tireless, putting away food for the winter. After a time, when enough was stored, she began going with Uhtatse on his work about the mesa, saying nothing to distract him, simply staying behind him, step for step, and taking comfort in his presence.

Autumn after autumn saw her disappear into the Women's House to a time of pain and loss. Uhtatse came to believe that she must be stronger than any person he had ever known, for she faced that without faltering, knowing that it must come inevitably. Her teeth began to rot, and the Healer chiseled the worst of them from her gums with a stone knife, and every time Uhtatse looked at her he felt sorrow for her burden.

Years passed, until they approached middle age. Each of them had now seen twenty-five winters, and they were the age of some who were about to become grandparents. A large part of their own contemporaries were gone already into death, taken by lung sickness or accident or in Kiyate raids. For every person of

Ki-shi-o-te's or the Old Woman's age, there were hundreds who never reached their thirtieth winter.

The Tsununni had not come. Still Uhtatse argued for moving their homes, but now it was because of the terrible winters, which seemed to grow worse with each passing year.

Yet still he was not comforted that the Tsununni remained unseen. He felt them, there beyond the edge of the world, lurking like some blizzard that was yet to arrive. They would come, he knew, and he only hoped that something would happen to make his people come to their senses before that time arrived.

He was thinking of that as he sat with Ki-shi-o-te, waiting with him yet again to hear that Ihyannah lived, after her yearly ordeal. Sihala was not with her daughter, now, for she had died the winter before, coughing her lungs up in bloody fragments. The old man himself was near death, his joints twisted painfully with arthritis, his fingers like claws, lying on a blanket in the shadow of the ancient juniper beside the doorway.

When Ahyallah came into view, she was carrying herself so strongly and buoyantly that Uhtatse felt his heart pound. He rose to greet her, puzzled that her expression was so eager. She didn't seem like one who had seen the death of an infant.

She smiled as she came up to him. "You have

a son," she said as he stared at her, dazzled by the news.

She bent over Ki-shi-o-te. "Old one, can you hear me?"

The ancient looked up through his clouded eyes, his wrinkles deepening with concentration. "I hear."

Ahyallah bent nearer still. "Ihyannah has given birth to a fine boy. A living child, strong and well formed."

Uhtatse was still reeling with the unexpected joy of the news, and he watched, amazed, as the old man struggled to sit up on his blanket. His gaze grew sharper, and something like his old spirit lit his furrowed face. For the first time in the months since Sihala's death, he seemed to see the world around him and to attend to what was said.

"A son? Alive?" he asked, his voice reedy but stronger than it had been for a long while.

Ahyallah nodded.

"What do the women wish to call him?" he asked, a pleading note in his voice.

It would have been Sihala's task to name the child, but she was gone. The correct thing would have been to leave that now to Ihyannah's aunt, but Ahyallah was a wise and compassionate woman. She felt that no important power would be offended if this single child, so long awaited, were named by his grandfather.

"They have not chosen," she said. "A suggestion might be welcome."

Ki-shi-o-te sighed. His eyes closed for a moment. His hands, parchment skin over long, fine bones and gnarled joints, clenched in his lap. Then he opened his eyes and said, with something of his old authority, "This child must be called Ka-shay-neet. The long-awaited one. If that pleases the women."

Ahyallah smiled. "A fine suggestion. I will tell them, and I am certain they will be grateful for help in this difficult naming."

Uhtatse, moving toward the Women's House, as if unable to control his feet, found himself in agreement. It was a fine name, well chosen. For a child . . . a child that was his and Ihyannah's!

It had been so long, their hopes so many times frustrated, that he could hardly believe in the fact of his son's existence. Best of all was the fact that Ihyannah had no living brother to do the things that were usually the duties of an uncle. He would be the one to teach his own son! He found himself grinning foolishly at a jay sitting on a juniper branch, a ground squirrel scuttering away into the piñons.

When he came in sight of the Women's House, he stopped. It was not proper for him to approach it at all. Still, he gazed, as if to look through the mud and lath walls, into the cramped space where his woman lay with her child.

As he stood there, beaming, Karenni came down the path. "I have felt our brother's joy," he said. "Come with me. Let us walk over the mesa. You will not sleep tonight, I know, and I will keep you company."

Uhtatse felt a huge smile taking shape upon his face. He said nothing, but he turned and followed Karenni through the junipers toward the cliff facing east, where the reddish moonlight turned the golden stone coppery. The air was fresh, for autumn's hem had already swept over the high country. A hint of the year's change scented the light breeze.

He stood beside Karenni, breathing deeply, feeling the distant mountains, their forests and their beasts, looming out of sight. He had never felt more joyful, even as a boy.

He turned to his sister's man. "Let us walk far tonight. My muscles need to work hard, or my happiness will lift me from this rock and into the sky. I would look out over the northwest plains."

Karenni seemed to stiffen. His head came up, and his nostrils flared in the dim light. "There is need for that," he said.

Something hard and cold formed in Uhtatse's gut. Was the time now? In the middle of this wonderful time, was the terror of the Tsununni coming upon his people? He turned his face toward the north and began to run, hearing Karenni keeping pace just behind him.

They arrived at the point from which the watchers surveyed the plain. The red moon was now low, staining the grasslands with light and shadow. Nothing visible moved there, yet Uhtatse felt motion. Distant motion, far beyond the horizon, almost beyond his perceptions. Yet something moved there, and its motion chilled him with foreboding.

Behind him, Karenni said softly, "I feel them. One who has suffered at their hands, as I have done, needs no great gift for that. I felt them living and breathing far beyond the mountains and the desert, for all these years.

"I feel them still, and they are closer now. They are not at our door, but they are nearer to us than I like having them. In time, they will find us, brother."

The One Who Smelled the Wind barely heard his words. All his senses were assaulting him with warnings. The wind, the grass, the beasts on the plains, the creatures in the mountains signalled him. Danger! He felt as if he were spread like a net on the air of the mesa, picking up in his meshes all those warnings from afar.

He stood for an hour, sensing. When he turned at last, Karenni waited patiently, his dark gaze fixed on the dimming countryside.

The moon had set.

"They are still very far away. It will be a long while before they reach us and even longer before they know we are here," he said to Karenni.

"They are like wolves. They can scent prey from very far away," the man replied. "They will smell new game, believe me, brother. They will come sooner than you think."

Uhtatse raised his chin toward the stars and gave a long, doleful shout. A wailing howl echoed it from the plain.

He turned to follow Karenni back toward their own pueblo. He could feel his new son, his triumphant wife ... their lives vibrated strongly in his heart, even from such a distance.

How long would they have to nurture their child in peace? Uhtatse felt with chilly certainty that it would not be long.

This, if nothing else, gave him an incentive to find a way to make his own people safe, if no one else. The Tsununni were nearer. Much nearer.

They would not kill his wife. They would not kill his son. He would find a way, no matter how difficult it might be, to protect them from this new and terrible enemy.

XXIII

Sitting in the chill evening, old Uhtatse shivered. His feet were numb now. His chest felt vaguely painful, and his vision seemed unusually dim.

Still, he didn't move. There was no need for him to return to the houses in the cliffs. No son awaited him there. No old wife puttered about her fire.

His life was moving past him, flowing away like a river into the deep canyons of time. If that life held pain, it also held great joy, and he knew that it was now his task to remember it to the end.

He sighed and shifted his weight from one painful hip to the other. He had not known so long ago how brief that time with his son would be. How little time, indeed, was left to his people in their pueblos on the mesa.

He closed his eyes against the piercing light of the stars, which seemed to sit very near the top of the mesa. Again he saw Ka-shay-neet and Ihyannah, together in the summer fields, snug in the winter house set into the cliff, singing their songs as they sat in the autumn evenings, waiting for the first cold blast from the north.

It always warmed him when he could call that vision into his mind. It did so now.

XXIV

Time passed, and the Tsununni did not come. The winters, however, grew colder, and the runoffs in spring swept away the little dams of the catchments and washed out large amounts of the precious soil they had gathered together in the gardens. Life, never easy, became an important fraction harder for the Ahye-tum-dat-sehe.

Uhtatse never stopped trying to persuade his people to shelter in the cliffs, though they no longer listened to him when he mentioned his plan. Then came the first of the Tsununni raids.

Spring had deepened into summer. The gardens were growing well, and every member of the clan was busy about some task.

Uhtatse, roaming from end to end of the mesa, met other Ones Who Smelled the Wind from the other clans, and each of them felt a subtle unease, though not one of the others was as powerful in his sensings as Uhtatse. His own feelings, always acute, had grown painful. Every scent on the breeze, every movement in the brush, as deer browsed or birds fed, impinged upon him sharply.

Something moved out on the lower country, and he knew it, feeling it inside as sharply as he felt his own movements. Karenni, too, knew.

"It is like an old wound that aches when the wind changes," he said to Uhtatse. "I have no talent such as yours. I cannot feel the bird fly or the deer leap, yet when the Tsununni move over the land, I know it. And they are moving now, drawing nearer and nearer to the mesa. I fear for us all. The Tsununni are terrible when they are angry—and they are always angry."

Uhtatse did not reply. What was there to say? But he redoubled his watchfulness, taking small naps from time to time as the days grew longer. He kept his alertness tuned to fever pitch.

Ka-shay-neet liked to follow him about his rounds. The boy was now old enough to pull weeds as his mother worked in the gardens, but from time to time Uhtatse allowed his son to go with him. He found himself happy that, for lack of a maternal uncle, he must be the child's teacher. He took much pleasure in that instruction, but not even when most involved did he allow himself to relax his vigilance.

So it was that as he stood on the promontory with his son, staring out over the grasslands, an undeniable sensing skewered him with pain. It struck with the impact of a stone or an arrow, and he flinched and reached for his son's hand. This was the thing he had feared for so long. This was the threat to his family that he had dreaded for years.

He turned and said, quite calmly, "Come. We must go to the Big House. There is danger in the lowlands, and it will come here."

Ka-shay-neet stared up, his black eyes bright with excitement. "Danger? The Kiyate? I have never seen them. Only the Anensi."

"Not the Kiyate," said Uhtatse. "Much worse. Tsununni."

The child knew the name, for he had listened from his bed place as his parents talked with Karenni for all the years of his short life. As if the name were a chill wind, he shivered and held tightly to his father's hand as the two strode across the drying summer grass. They hurried through the stands of piñon and juniper, toward the pueblo his people shared.

Ki-shi-o-te had rallied at the birth of his grandson. He was now so ancient that only the Old Woman Who Sang the Future might call him her junior, and he spent his days sitting in the sun, warming his frail bones in a clear space near the pueblo.

Uhtatse saw his grizzled head lift as the pair drew near, though he knew that his father-in-law could see little with his clouded eyes.

"You smell of fear and danger," said the old

man. His gray-webbed pupils strained toward Uhtatse. "What have you sensed, Uhtatse?"

The younger man knelt in the dust beside the old one. He took the hand, all bones and shrunken skin, that Ki-shi-o-te held out to him and held it between his own. In the distance, someone played a reed flute, the quavering notes rising into the air with painful clarity. Uhtatse would never again hear a flute played without recalling that day with unhappy vividness.

"Tsununni," he said, his voice quiet. "Not far enough away. Three days, at the most, will bring them to the mesa, and it is in this direction that they come. If Karenni is correct, they will then be upon us, angry as wasps whose nest has been robbed of grubs."

The old man reached convulsively to take the hand of his grandson. "Ohayeeeyeh!" he mourned softly. "Our people! Our people! Go and warn the Ahye-tum-datsehe, my son. Let Ka-shay-neet stay here to comfort my spirit."

Now Uhtatse had lived for long enough to know that people did not always believe in the things they had always seemed to understand. Ha-no-na-say had none of the perceptiveness his predecessor had held, and he had not truly believed in the abilities of the One Who Smelled the Wind, no matter that storms had been predicted and sickness among the animals in the Middle Way had been warned of so as to prevent the people from eating tainted game.

Now he found the Teacher as he sat with the elders, weaving in the kiva. They all looked up, startled to see him here at midday. He saw in the Teacher's eyes the shock of recognition even before he spoke. Ha-no-na-say had not believed—but now he knew his error.

"The Tsununni are on the plain. Three days away, no more. They will come here, for this is their direction. Karenni says that they scent prey, as does the wolf, with terrible accuracy. We will seem to be easy victims to them, for they have fought the most powerful tribes in the flatlands and they have won."

The dark faces, shining with oil in the heat of the kiva and the light of the fire, turned toward him, frozen into stillness. Hands went quiet on their work, eyes veiled themselves as those old ones who held the welfare of their tribe accepted his words.

"These are not the Kiyate," said the Healer at last. "We do not know their ways. They do not know ours. There will be terrible bloodshed. We must take thought for the safety of the very young and the ill and the ancients. We must make more weapons, harvest what we can of the crops, and hide the food in invisible clefts in the rock."

Uhtatse could see near panic in the man's eyes. "We need weeks! We have three days!"

"Perhaps three days," said the One Who Smelled the Wind. "Possibly even less. We must place more watchers . . . the other clans will help in this. Send runners to tell them what I have seen and to ask for men to be set on the promontories."

Ha-no-na-say turned to the small boy who always lingered about the opening into the kiva in order to run errands for the old ones. "Go and find See-tan-tahay. Bring him to us here. Run!"

Then he rose to stand facing Uhtatse. "I was wrong," he said. "For all these years, I have been wrong. The danger has come, and if we had done as you asked, all our people would have been safe in the caves in the cliffs. The ways could be made secret so that strangers would not know how to set their feet in order to be able to go and come all the way. One warrior could hold each cave. It would be so easy to defend. . . . " He caught himself.

"But it is too late to think of that. We must arrange safety for our people. Uhtatse, what do you suggest?"

XXV

Uhtatse sighed. "My winter house, down in the side of the cliff, is small, but it can hold the very youngest of the children. One woman can guard it easily, with another to comfort the young ones. The larger children can shelter in the cave around the walls. . . . The niche is, I think, large enough for all of them. Any who might try to come there would not walk away again. And who would know where to look, except one of our own?"

Ha-no-na-say nodded sadly. "If the Tsununni are to come here, we will have to move, as you have said so often, into the cliffsides. It is too late, now, to do anything but safeguard the young."

A voice interrupted them. The boy called down from the opening, "See-tan-tahay is here! And the Old Woman, too. She asks you to come up, so that she may talk with you."

The elders moved stiffly to climb the ladder

into the warm day. Sometimes the prohibition against women visiting the kiva was a nuisance, and today was one of those times. But all the houses belonged to the women, and the men felt that there must be some single spot that was theirs alone.

She waited while Ha-no-na-say sent the runner on his way with the message for the tribes. Then she leaned toward the Teacher, her faded eyes glimmering with excitement.

"We need a new strategy. These are not the Kiyate, and they will not fight in the ways we know. They will not know what to expect of us, but if they have fought with others who live in pueblos, they will expect us to shelter there. We of the women can defend the deep rooms, as we have always done, but without really intending to keep the attackers out.

"If these are like the Kiyate, they will want to sweep through our house, destroying what they cannot take with them. We will let ourselves be brushed aside, as if we were weaker than we are. We shall let them into the Big House ... "

Uhtatse caught her thought, a flame of excitement now building inside him. "And we will come in behind them, trapping them in the small rooms and the passages, killing them like turkeys as they squawk and flap in the trap!" he exclaimed. "We can seal many of the outer doors, so that they cannot get away."

Then he took thought of his own limitations. "I will stand aside, keeping my own hands free of blood, so that my gift will not desert my people. But the plan will work, and it should give the Tsununni reason to think hard before coming again to our mesa."

The thought of something new, an element in warfare that they had never seen before, caught the imaginations of the elders. When they took the idea to the members of the clan, it put new vigor into their preparations for battle. The three days went too quickly, but when they had passed, the mesa was very far from being in its usual state.

Uhtatse moved tirelessly from south to north, east to west, feeling the approach of the enemy and warning all the clans to prepare as his own had done. The multitude of emotions, so different from the ordinary ones, frustrated his attempts to feel the enemy as precisely as he would have liked, but he strained to know their nearness.

When he came to the last outpost, far out on a point of rock that extended above a deep cleft, he found the first sign that he had missed some of the enemy's scouts. There he found the first communication from the Tsununni.

Two men had occupied the watch post. They were in their places, pinned into position by sharpened stakes that had been thrust through their flesh into crevices in the stone.

Their eyeballs gazed lidlessly over the lowlands, still watching. Their tongues had been removed, so their spirits could never tell what they had seen.

Uhtatse's heart seemed to freeze, his breath chilling in his lungs. How had he failed to feel the agony of these men as they died? He had been busy with many concerns, but their deaths should have sliced cleanly through all of those.

He focused his senses upon the area about him, that below the outthrust stone. He felt even ants moving in their below-ground runnels. But he felt no trace of the enemy. Whoever had killed these men was no longer here.

Even as he strained to feel any trace of the Tsununni, he bent over the dead men, trying to learn how they had died. Then he understood why he had not felt their passing.

Each had been killed instantly, one with a knife stroke through his back, one with a spear thrust through his side and into his heart. He shivered, thinking of men capable of creeping up on watchmen as skilled as these, as alert as they had been.

Then he was running. On the fringes of his mind, he felt men moving in the Middle Way. They were all too near the pueblo of his own people, and he knew that they would find passable routes to the tops of the cliffs.

XXVI

He went bounding through the juniper forest like a frightened deer. Ha-no-na-say's guards called as he ran, and he shouted warnings to them without pausing. He wanted to see with his own eyes that the children were safe in Ihyannah's winter house. He wanted to touch Ihyannah's hand once more. When war came, there was no certainty of any future for anyone.

Others had spotted the Tsununni's movements in the Middle Way. Already, the children were sheltered in the niche about the house. Umeya, his sister, was one of the women assigned to defend them.

Many short spears, loosely grouped in bundles, were ready to hand. Clubs with long handles and knotted heads leaned against the walls of the cave as well. Any warrior attempting the descent into that niche, with its even more perilous swing around the buttress rock into the house place, would find himself faced with instant death.

This was a place that a single person could guard for as long as water and food remained at hand, and for a considerable time after that.

The children were huddled between the end of the house and the curve of the rear wall of the cranny. Nineteen small faces looked up as Uhtatse came down the cliff. He called to his sister as he moved to swing into the niche. Kashay-neet was waiting for him as his feet touched the stone.

Uhtatse reached for the child's warm hand and stood holding on to it for a moment. Kashay-neet stared up into his father's eyes. Much passed between the pair of them without a word being spoken, and then the boy turned and rejoined the other children. There was no more time for feelings. This was the time for war.

Uhtatse smiled at his sister, though he knew that smile was more of a grimace. Umeya's, in return, was little better. The two women were naked, their skins oiled, and their hair tied back with juniper-bark strings to be out of their way. He pitied anyone who came here to threaten their charges.

He climbed back to the mesa top in better spirits. Ihyannah waited there for him, pausing in her work of piling dry juniper and piñon branches beside the doorways of the Big House.

She gripped his hands tightly for an instant, and then both returned to their work.

Uhtatse and Karenni, between them, had persuaded the Ahye-tum-datsehe that their usual tactics would not help them against the Tsununni. Those people did not abide by anyone's rules for warfare. The almost-choreographed ritual battles with the Kiyate were of no use as experience to a people faced with this new enemy.

"We must learn new ways of fighting," Karenni had urged them as soon as their peril was obvious.

After the Old Woman's brilliant proposal had been worked into a usable plan, others had come forward with original and useful ideas. As he moved about, helping where he could, Uhtatse saw preparations made ready for using many of those new notions. It was some comfort to know that the Tsununni were not attacking a people who were too set in their old ways to learn new ones when the need was upon them.

The sun was now setting. The movement in the Middle Way was disturbing the deer and frightening the birds and small animals. What were they doing, those alien people, as they prepared to attack?

As darkness fell, he began to understand, for his own people were chanting prayers to the gods, beating softly on the skin drums and sending the shrill notes of the bone-and-reed flutes to rise on the air as an offering. Those others were probably calling upon their own fierce deities to help them in their attack.

No one fought at night. It would have been foolish of the Tsununni, who were never foolish, to come upon a people they did not know, in a place unfamiliar to them, in the darkness. While night held sway, there would be no battle. But Uhtatse knew that dawn would find matters terribly changed.

The Ahye-tum-datsehe danced on the roofs of the kivas, all over the joined mesas. The women circled, arms linked, while the men stamped out defiant rhythms. Down below, were their enemies making their own rituals, propitiating their own gods? The thought did not comfort him.

The stars were cold, frozen into the black sky. The heights beyond the canyon were dark bulks raised against the spangled breadth of the heavens. A streak of fire was traced, for an instant, against the moonless blackness, and Uhtatse caught his breath. An omen!

Of what kind? Was it a sign of hope for his people, or was it a signal of victory for those others below? He felt, even through his own wonder and fear, an echo of those feelings from other hearts. The Tsununni, too, had seen. They, too, were wondering what that bright signal might mean.

He sighed and rose from the rock where he was sitting. It was time to return to the people.

They had not missed him. The dancing went

on, steady and rhythmic, almost hypnotic. Ki-shi-o-te had been brought to sit beside the fire, lending his ancient authority to the pleas of his people. The Old Woman sat beside him, making even one as old as Ki-shi-o-te look compara-tively young by contrast.

Ha-no-na-say sat with the elders, resting from dancing, his place taken for a time by a younger man. When Uhtatse joined them, they did not seem to notice. They were completely focused upon bringing the help of the gods—the god of thunder and lightning, the god of snow, that of making the plants and animals prosper and grow—to the aid of their own.

The One Who Smelled the Wind was apart from those things. He watched, but he did not compel or participate. Uhtatse sat quietly, rest-ing and waiting.

When at last the dancing ended, the stars were turning pale in the east. A line of lighter color traced itself along the eastern line of the horizon.

This was the day of war.

XXVII

Before there was light for seeing, the fires were quenched. The women slipped away through the darkness to their posts about and in the pueblo, and the men made certain that their pots containing coals of fire were fed and stoppered against future need. Then they, too, went to their positions, hidden in the rough tangles of juniper, the runnels of washes, the shallow canyons, and the crannies in the soil of the mesa.

With the lightening of the sky, there came motion among the stunted trees. A blade of grass was crushed with an almost inaudible sound, but Uhtatse heard it. A branch of piñon brushed gently over an oiled and painted face, and the One Who Smelled the Wind heard the sound and smelled the infinitesimal bruising of the needles, the disturbed paint.

He reached out, as he had told his people that he would do, to ask the morning hawk to shrill its cry, and the bird skree'd raucously from on high. That was his warning to the Ahye-tum-datsehe. Now they knew that the Tsununni were among them.

When he was certain that no more warriors were left to pass his position, he slithered across the ground with the agility of a lizard toward an upthrust boulder from which he would be able to see—and more important, feel—the battle to come. He could not kill with his hands, but he hoped that he might give warning of danger from an unexpected quarter, if such came upon his people.

He curled his body against the rock, keeping his head low to remain invisible to those now approaching the pueblo. Even as he watched, there came a high-pitched cry from among the junipers and the whispery sound of lances cast from the atlatl; the whoosh of arrows loosed from twanging bowstrings broke the stillness of the dawn.

A chorus of women's voices shrilled, chants and imprecations and threats all mingling together, drawing the Tsununni irresistibly toward the guarded house where those who dwelt in Big Houses always put their young in time of need. Now Uhtatse closed his eyes, for the light was still too tenuous for seeing clearly, and focused his attention upon one of the invaders.

The man was crawling, his knees and hands prickling over the stickery debris beneath the trees. His heart was racing with fierce pleasure as he rose and loosed an arrow toward the dark bulk of the pueblo. Even as he moved forward, something sped from the shadowy bulk and buried itself in his heart. Uhtatse felt his wondering mind fail to accept his death, even as it came upon him. Then the One Who Smelled the Wind withdrew and found another viewpoint from which to follow the attack.

He found Ihyannah, who crouched beside the door toward which the warriors came. He could feel the bow in her hands, the arrow already nocked between her fingers. She loosed the shaft, and before it was fairly clear, she had another in its place. Then a dark shape leaped from the shadows and clubbed her down.

Ihyannah! But she lived; he was sure before he went forward with the line of attackers.

They were making their way to the pueblo now, with some difficulty but far more ease, as the Kiyate could have told them, than they should have done. The doorway was a blacker shape against the dark wall, and then the man through whose eyes Uhtatse saw was darting through it . . . only to be knocked senseless by one of the useful clubs. This one was wielded by the midwife herself.

With deliberation, the women allowed the Tsununni to force them aside and to penetrate the inner rooms of the pueblo. As the attackers passed them, the defenders slipped out of the house, taking with them those who had been wounded or knocked senseless.

Now it was light enough for Uhtatse to see with his eyes the progress of the battle. The last of the women came out of the pueblo, and at once they began cramming dead brush into the opening. One of the pots of coals was flung into the heap, and smoke began to rise as groups of armed people moved to right and left about the house, going to cover the door that had been left unsealed at the rear.

He tensed, hoping that in the excitement they had not built the fires too high and endangered the juniper stringers, but he relaxed when he saw wet hides being spread over the flaming piles of wood. Thick smoke boiled up out of the door, and he knew that it was also being drawn into the rooms and up through the smoke holes in the ceilings of the layered chambers.

He waited, with his people, for the smoke to take effect. A commotion beyond the corner told him that some of the Tsununni were trying to fight their way out of the pueblo. And then Ihyannah, who had regained consciousness, and Ha-no-na-say reached into the door with long poles and pulled the fires out onto the trodden dirt. Without waiting, a group of men, armed with flint knives and stone hatchets, ran into the blackness.

Now there was too much darkness and smoke and confusion for Uhtatse to know anything, even through the eyes of one in the house. He must wait still, clenching his fists against his impatience, until someone emerged from that turmoil to report what had taken place.

Then he froze in place. Others behind him! He turned to see dark shapes running lightly through the juniper wood.

"O-hay-ay-ay-ay-yah!" he shouted, and Karenni turned toward him from his position beside the house. He saw the new danger at once and yelled in turn to those behind the pueblo and those concealed about the grounds.

Uhtatse dropped behind the rock, as a short spear clattered where he had been lying. He heard a whiz of arrows go overhead toward the approaching Tsununni, and then his own people were there, taking cover behind the stones and sending a hail of missiles and spears toward the reserve group of enemies.

Uhtatse rose to his full height and gazed over the boulder at those who were now pinned down in the wood. They were fearful to see. They had painted their faces in alternate stripes of black and ocher, with round patches about the eyes that looked like the gaping eye holes of skulls. Their bodies, too, were striped, each in his own pattern of zigzags or curves, and even face-to-face they were hard to distinguish from the shadows of the branches on the pale soil.

He felt the breeze against his cheek as a spear passed his face, but he did not move. He could not kill them but he could stand against them in his flesh and his mind, holding their attention while his people circled to get behind them.

There came a terrible yell from the direction of the pueblo, mixed with the cries of women who were roused to great anger. He did not turn to see, though Karenni, now beside him, did.

"They come," said his brother.

Then there was the swift thud of moccasined feet against the ground and the grunts of stressed lungs as striped men dashed past the tumble of rocks toward the Tsununni pinned down in the junipers. Uhtatse and his people let them pass. There would be captives back at the Big House, he knew. These could find their way into the plains again, taking with them word that the Ahye-tum-datsehe were not to be attacked lightly on their mesa.

Perhaps when they came again, the People would be sheltered in new homes, less accessible to attack than these. When they again climbed the ways onto the mesa, the Tsununni would be met with a situation with which even they would not know how to deal.

XXVIII

Though it had seemed to pass as swiftly as the shadow of a cloud over the Middle Way, the battle had lasted for almost half the day. The Tsununni had melted down the cliff, and Uhtatse felt more than one of them fall to his death from the precipitous cleft up which they had climbed. Others of the enemy lay dead among the trees and in and around the pueblo.

He turned, weary now, toward the Big House and picked his way among the wounded and the dead to find Ihyannah. She stood with Kosiah and the Old Woman and the Teacher, all of them bending over a quiet shape. Uhtatse felt his heart lurch.

It was Ki-shi-o-te. He had hidden among the junipers, and when the Tsununni came he attacked them with his short lance, which was still gripped firmly in his withered hand. He had died face-to-face with his enemy, as he would have chosen to do, going into the Other

Place as a warrior, not as an ancient who was unable to stand or to help himself.

Uhtatse touched his wife's arm, and she turned to him, her eyes dry and her gaze strangely triumphant. "He went well, my father," she said.

He nodded, feeling in his heart a great emptiness where his old friend had lived. "Our son will be proud of him," he returned. "We will give him to the fire, with his fellow warriors, and his bones will be kept in a jar in our house to remind us of him."

She drew a deep breath. He felt from her a wave of joy, as if the battle and the death of her suffering father had lifted from her shoulders a great burden. "Our son will light the pyre, if that is fitting," she suggested.

It was fitting. And that reminded Uhtatse of the children, huddled in the cliff. He sent the runner to bring up those who had remained below, as the rest began tending wounds and taking the dead to the place where the pyre would be built.

There were three Tsununni left alive, and those had been unconscious when taken captive, or they, too, would have died. Ha-no-na-say had them bound tightly, so they could not run off the cliff to their deaths, and put on the top of the biggest kiva. When the dead were sent to the sun, there would be time for their attackers.

Night found the dead arranged neatly together upon a bed of layered deadwood. It was not fitting to send them to the sun in the darkness, so chants were sung all night, weary though the Ahye-tum-datsehe might be, and the youngest children danced for them, as the adults were still busy repairing the damage to the Big House.

There was little rest that night, and the stimulus of battle had long since worn away, leaving bones weary and eyes heavy. Before dawn, all slept for a short while, leaving Uhtatse to watch the mesa.

He walked, to keep from falling asleep, along the edge of the cliff, staring down into the dark gulf below. They would not come that way again, he thought, having learned that this prey were not so stupid as to think the route impossible. Only those used to living in flatter country would suppose that a mountain-reared kind would not walk up and down the heights and know that others could do so as well.

The night wore away, and he was thankful that it was not the one before it, with all this suffering and death yet to come. When the first light touched the east, he turned and ran toward his own people's house, chanting a breathless rhythm all the way. It contained thanks to the gods and praise for the fallen and hope for the future, all twined together into its plaintive melody.

The people were rising when he arrived, gathering damaged goods together, checking for breakage and spillage in the storage rooms, getting ready for the feast that would accompany the burning of the dead. They had already pushed the dead Tsununni over the cliff, condemning their spirits to endless wandering with the winds instead of the assurance of the Other Place, and only the rites for their own fallen remained to do.

That took place at sunrise, and the Old Woman Who Sang the Future, the Old Man Who Dreamed the Past, the Teacher, the Healer, and Uhtatse stood together amid the people, waiting. Ka-shay-neet, his eyes wide and his small face serious with his great responsibility, held a burning brand. His hand did not shake as he listened to the chant.

His mother nodded to him at last, and the boy went to the pyre and thrust the blaze into the dry wood. He remained there, squinting against the smoke and sparks, until the pile was well kindled. Then he reached far up to touch the robe in which his grandfather was wrapped.

The two had been close, and Uhtatse knew that the child was sore of heart, though he showed no sign of it as he turned back to stand with his mother, watching his people burn and return to the Other Place, where the sun lived. The child had the pride of his family in him, and his father was filled with quiet satisfaction as he watched the flames curl up around the wrapped bodies and he breathed the rank smoke of their burning.

The pillar rose into the sky, marking the spot for those Tsununni who were even now moving out onto the lower country. Uhtatse felt their fury, even so far away, as he had felt their approach. He felt also the resigned despair of those captives awaiting the attention of this mesa people, who were not so weak as they had supposed them to be.

When the burning was done, it would be time to deal with those. They might live for days, and the fury and frustration of the Ahye-tum-datsehe would make their departure from life a painful matter, indeed.

Though he said nothing, he knew that he would suffer, with them, every torment the women devised. It was a part of his gift, and he could not shut away those things he did not wish to feel without shutting away those he must know for the safety of his people.

Today would be a terrible day for all of them, he knew, and he smiled at his family and his fellows and said nothing of it to anyone. He would endure, as he had before, what was necessary and still he would be Uhtatse, the One Who Smelled the Wind.

XXIX

The old man sitting on the cliff shivered as the wind bit through his wrappings. But it was not only the cold that went to his heart. He still recalled the entertainment the women of the Ahye-tum-datsehe had given those captives so many seasons ago.

He had attended, of course, for a time. When it had become unbearable for him to remain, he had slipped away into the junipers to find his old place, where he had purified his hands of blood. In some way, it seemed that it might purify him of the terrible anger his people were giving vent to, there beside the fires.

Uhtatse did not frown. Not by the faintest tensing of a muscle or wrinkling of a line in his face did he reveal the torment he felt as the skins of the captives were deftly peeled or scorched or slivered with cactus thorns. He was an elder of his people, and he refused to let pain affect him.

It was not, indeed, the pain itself that tortured him now. It was the fury . . . the boiling rage that roared through the hearts of his people and lapped at the walls of his own spirit. Such anger was almost as damaging to his gift as the spilling of blood, and he walked blindly in its grip.

His feet carried him to the spot that he remembered with awe and thankfulness. The sharp outcrop over the canyon still protected the difficult way down the cliff face, and the light showed him the crannies he had used as a young man to work his way down into that sheltering niche, where he had loosed his weaknesses and his guilts.

So. This was what he must do while he wore out the lives of the Tsununni with them.

He dropped his sandals on the stone, dusted his fingers with grit, and started down the precipice. It had changed little, that climb, since he had left the place on the day his predecessor had died. Now he went swiftly as a lizard to find the cranny in which he had stood.

It had enlarged. A slab of sandstone had fallen away into the canyon, leaving a space sufficient for his greater size. He no longer had to cramp his elbows to his sides and keep his arms before him. He could stand erect, hands hanging loose beside him, and stare out over the space beyond.

He held himself rigid, holding in the blossoming agony within him. They were pausing now to refresh the victims. Allowed to suffer thirst and hunger, they would not last long enough for full satisfaction. It gave him time to feel the raging blisters, the raw weals, and skinless spaces left on the bodies of those distant men.

They were, he realized, men. Not animals, not simple predators. If he had been born a Tsununni, he understood with sudden clarity, he would have been precisely like those now dying for the guilt of their fellows. It was a strange thought, but before he had the time to examine it closely enough the pause was over, and the torture had begun again.

The sun moved over the mesa and down into the west. Still the Tsununni did not die—truly, they were a tough breed, those men of the plains. Still Uhtatse stood in his cranny in the cliff, learning again the ways of pain and thirst and the disciplines that ignored the flesh.

The night crawled past, but he paid no heed to the moon, which stared into his eyes. He was again entering that state of altered awareness that had gripped him before, when he stood in that place. He was moving out of his body, away from the mesa, even apart from the swallows and the hawks, the deer and the cats that lived there.

He seemed to see for a great distance over the lower places that lay about the mesa. Forests far greater than those formed by the little trees he knew rolled over masses of mountains toward the east. The plains to the west and north held cliffs to equal his own, and huge shapes of stone loomed over lands that were dry and desertlike.

He went higher yet, seeming to see, in his mind, that great water that Ra-onto had told him about as a lad. And the cities in the south, where men lived inside mesas . . .

After this day, he would have no trouble in persuading his own to take advantage of their own cliffs, he knew, but the thought was distant and unimportant as he let his mind go free on the wind, higher and higher, like an eagle or a hawk.

He was wrenched back into his flesh not by pain but by the ending of it. One sharp agony skewered his heart, as he came to himself. And then there was nothing where those lives had been. So. It was done.

How many days and nights had he stood in the cliff, waiting? He shook himself, flexed his hands, brought his feet back to life, and turned to climb again to his own place. The way seemed long, and an owl mourned as he came again into the night atop the mesa. He could feel its harsh gaze as it regarded him. He could feel the mouse just beginning to digest in its gut.

So he had cleansed himself yet again. The ending of the captives would not mean the end of his usefulness to his people, and that was good.

He ran toward the pueblo, the kiva where the people danced while the enemy suffered, the fires where the women had heated their instruments of torture. Ihyannah met him, somehow feeling his approach, and Ka-shay-neet was with her, his eyes wide, gleaming dark even in the night.

Uhtatse felt toward his son. Then he flinched backward, internally, from the pain that filled the child's spirit.

"You, too," he whispered, taking the boy's hand.

"They hurt!" the child whimpered. "They hurt, oh terribly, my father! They were bad men, but we did bad things to them!"

Ihyannah made an impatient gesture. "Say nothing!" she admonished her son. "Bad things sometimes have good results, though it is hard to understand that when you are small. Come with your father and me. We will go home to our little house. We will sleep all together, touching each other, knowing that we all live and are not dead like so many others.

"Bad things beget bad things. Never forget that. It does not make any of them right, but it makes them understandable."

Uhtatse stared at her shape against the paler sky as she led the way toward their own path down the cliff. He had never realized that she, too, thought of things like that. She had taken part unflinchingly in the torment of the Tsununni, he knew.

Had she, too, suffered with those she tortured, going forward with her duty because it was the way of her people? Had her own heart felt smothered in blood and pain? He wondered, as they went to their own place, at her courage and control. He had thought only of his own over the years, and now it occurred to him that his woman had her own sort, and it might be even more difficult to maintain than his could be.

They built a small blaze in the fire pit, not because it was cool, for the night was warm, but because all three needed its comfort. They huddled together, arms about each other, and watched the little flames dance among the sticks until they grew sleepy.

They rested at last in a tumble of warmth, and Uhtatse dreamed of nothing at all, though he had feared his own dreams as he stood in the cliff. Only calm darkness waited for him in sleep, however, and he went forward into it gladly.

Without comment, the Ahye-tum-datsehe be-gan building houses in the cliff caves. Uhtatse said nothing, either, only helping them to plan the layout of dwellings and kivas, of small homes and complex ones. He and Ihyannah were the only ones on the mesa with experience at living in the cliffsides, and their advice was constantly sought.

Ha-no-na-say had taken to heart his stub-bornness in resisting the change. He knew that many deaths could have been prevented if the People had been sheltered so, and Uhtatse could not argue against that. It was quite true. Now the Teacher was in the forefront of the planning, though he was too busy with teach-ing the young ones to labor for long at a time at cutting sandstone or letting the bulky blocks down the cliffs.

Others shared out their work in the fields or hunting for plants on the mesa and in the Middle Way. Hunters cooperated, making time for some to take part in the great work. Children too young for other work ran errands or held on to ropes or poured water for their elders, who toiled at the work.

It was not a task they expected to complete in a year, or even several years. One house or one complex at a time, they set the walls together, cut and cured the juniper for stringers, made the roofs, and set them onto the houses. The smallest houses were, of course, completed fairly quickly, and by the first winter ten families had moved down into the cliffs.

Uhtatse did what he could to help with the building in the summer, and in winter he and Ihyannah and Ka-shay-neet twisted rope as they sat beside their fire pit, talking and dreaming the terrible days away. By spring, it was agreed among all the Ahye-tum-datsehe that if there were no Tsununni at all, the increasing severity of the winters would drive them to move as quickly as possible to live down in the caves.

The One Who Smelled the Wind grew older, and many of those who had been his friends as a child died and were sent into the Other Place. Accidents, illnesses, infections ... many things preyed upon his people, and by the time Ka-shay-neet had counted ten summers, Uhtatse and Ihyannah were among those who were the elders of the tribe.

There was still the Old Woman Who Sang the

Future, of course. She seemed immortal, tough and brown and wrinkled as a dead root, still able to sing her visions for those who dared to ask for them, and acerbic as ever in her speech. Ha-no-na-say was a handful of summers older than Uhtatse, and the Healer a bit older than that. In all, there were perhaps a dozen of the Ahye-tum-datsehe who might be called truly old, counting six or seven double handfuls of summers to their credit. The rest had gone, and only regular births kept the population sufficient for survival.

Ihyannah no longer made a yearly visit to the Women's House. After the birth of her son, she no longer became pregnant, which was a great relief to Uhtatse. What she felt about it, she never said, though he often surprised a wistful look on her weathered face as she gazed after his sister Umeya's ever-increasing troop of young.

Almost all the People were now housed in the cliffsides, and those still living in pit houses or parts of the old pueblos seemed content to remain there for as long as they lived. They were among the older people, most of them, and changes were matters they had no patience to make. Their arthritic limbs, too, made the cliff paths difficult for them, so it was as well.

At night, there were glimmers of light from the many fire pits sprinkled against the farside cliffs, where those belonging to other tribes had imitated his own people. All over the mesa, the clans had seen the wisdom of that move and had gone to work to shelter themselves as Uhtatse's people had done. If the Tsununni came back again, they would find a very different situation from that one they had found before.

They did not approach the mesa again for a long while, though Uhtatse sensed them several times as they moved over distant parts of the lower country. Every time, he alerted the tribes, but never did the enemy come near enough to pose a threat.

Ka-shay-neet grew quicker and brighter from day to day, it seemed to his father. He was a talented bowman at a very early age, and he kept up the use of the atlatl as well, though that old-fashioned weapon was going out of use. He worked in the fields, helping his mother with her plants, and Uhtatse often wondered if this son of his might one day need to cleanse his own spirit of the deaths of weeds and plants, as he had done.

For it seemed that the boy had much of his parent's ability to read the unseen creatures of the mesa. He could sense the deer as they browsed, the rabbits as they crouched in their burrows, even the turkeys about their everlasting gabbling business of eating everything in sight.

To-ho-pe-pe had lived long enough to make a pet for the boy, his great age making a wonder to Uhtatse and Ihyannah. At his death, Ka-shay-neet had asked for his feathers, and from them he had made a cloak like wings, with the feathers sewed onto the deer hide in layers. In winter, his small figure, draped in that unlikely garment, was very funny, though strangely enough, none of the other children ever laughed at him.

Ki-shi-o-te, before his death, had said many times that his grandson had the potential to become one of the great men of his tribe. And yet every time, the old man had frowned, as if something troubled his mind. Uhtatse had asked, more than once, if he foresaw anything strange when he looked so, but he would shrug and shake his white head. Yet Uhtatse had a feeling still that the elder had seen some untoward thing in the future of his son.

And now the people were safe in the cliffs. Uhtatse had released some of the tense watchfulness he had felt since the birth of the boy, for the dangers that threatened him now were only those familiar ones that everyone on the mesa knew and did not think about.

Visiting from house to house was not as quick or as easy as it had been in the days when all had lived together in the pueblos. So when Kashay-neet did not come home one fall evening, neither his father nor his mother thought anything amiss. He had stayed with other families before, as their children had stayed in his mother's house. That was nothing to cause concern.

Uhtatse climbed the cliff the next morning without worry. Karenni hailed him as he came with Na-to-si from an early hunt in the Middle Way.

"Did the boy come to you for the night?" asked Uhtatse as he gained his foothold and faced them.

"Yes. He will be a fine hunter one day," said Na-to-si. "He and my own son planned a rabbit hunt for today, and they left when I did. There will be rabbit for the cook pots tonight, I suspect, for they both know what they are doing."

The One Who Smelled the Wind smiled and went about his business of guarding the mesa. Nothing whispered to him that today would see the end of his happiness. The breeze did not hint that it was seeing the last of his son.

But in early afternoon, Uhtatse paused as if shot to the heart, bending with the pain of the invisible arrow in his chest. "Ahhhhh!" he moaned, trying to get his breath.

He felt a sense of falling, there beyond the old pueblo. Fear wrapped that mind that linked with his. And then there was nothing but pain, shattering pain, and sudden blackness.

"Ka-shay-neet!" he shouted, drawing himself up and beginning to run. "Ka-shay-neet!"

But there was no answer, ever, to his anguished cry.

XXXI

Even now, after many hands of years, the memory of that moment filled the ancient Uhtatse with pain. Others lost children, of course, yet most had others to comfort their hearts. He and Ihyannah had no child left, though he had tried to put all his energy into working with his sisters' children.

Ihyannah had no such outlet, and she had grown silent, her face seeming to wither like a winter-killed flower. He remembered his frustration, wrapped in his own grief, at his inability to help to conquer hers.

The sun was long down, and the bitter night rattled the icy twigs of the juniper above his head. It was no colder than the little house in the cliff, which he had shared with the mother of his son. Try as they might to generate a warmth between them once again, they seemed separated by a wall of stone—or of ice—that held them apart in their separate griefs.

*Now the old man bent his face into his hands.
That other memory, which was in its way as
terrible as that of Ka-shay-neet's death, had
come walking into his mind. It was one that
wracked him and had done so for many seasons.*

Uhtatse moved silently among the junipers,
absorbing the fragrant stillness of the morning.
He slipped past browsing deer, chipmunks, and
kangaroo rats sunning themselves on their tiny
doorsteps. He was going about his work,
breathing deeply the scents of the new day and
listening to the skree of the north-quarter
hawk.

The texture of the air moved in quiet ripples
across his skin, bringing with it all the matters
moving upon the mesa. Something—a scent? a
sound?—made his skin ridge suddenly into
goose pimples. It was not a sign of any enemy,
he knew. The creatures of the high places were
undisturbed.

No. It was something else.

His son . . . and then he remembered. There
would be no sign of his son, ever again. They
had not found his small body, search as they
might, but his spirit had not come to haunt his
father. Uhtatse longed to believe that by some
strange quirk of the gods, he had gone to the
Other Place, without the help of the ritual.

No, he was at his work on the mesa. He
should spare no time for his own concerns. Yet

there was something . . . the air was tinged with a hint of something familiar that should not be where it was now.

The hawk now saw something and stooped to check on it. There was a faint query in his cry as he called from above: something that he saw interested him without causing him any fright.

Uhtatse turned away from his work and went to the edge of the cliff. He stared up and down the adjacent canyon. Below him, swallows dipped and swooped above the deeps, with more joining them from the nests filling the tiny crannies in the face of the cliff.

Theirs was an intricate dance, filling his eyes with motion even as their burbling cries filled his ears with sound. Amid that he suddenly heard another sound, faint in the distance.

It was a song . . . a long quavering song and a familiar voice that filled his spirit with terror.

He turned to run along the irregular edge of the precipice. There was a point of rock extending over the canyon. From that spot, he could see the edge in both directions, and he ran toward it with all his speed and strength, forgetting prudence in his haste.

Somewhere inside him there was a sudden dread that grew as he went forward. That was a deathsong that he heard. That familiar voice was chanting the words to the morning sky.

He reached the point and broke through a thin screen of trees. He stared along the cliff toward the source of the sound . . .

She sat on a slender spur of stone, below and some distance to his right. He knew the place. It was very hard to reach it without risking a fatal fall into the canyon below. There was no way to reach her now, and Ihyannah sat serenely, looking out over the gulf as she sang.

Uhtatse almost cried out, but he caught the sound between his teeth and ground it to silence. She was sitting in the shadow of the cliff, and the rising sun was painting the distant walls beyond the canyon with golden light. She, however, was gazing into some place not lit by suns.

He stood waiting, quieting the thunder of his heart. He wanted desperately to call out to her, but that was not his right. She was alone with her Mystery, and he must abide by her decision, though it left him bereft, indeed.

She knew that he was there. He understood that, although he did not know how it was that she felt his presence. She lifted a hand, palm out, toward the spot where he stood, in both apology and farewell.

When she rose to her feet, he tried to close his eyes, but he could not manage to do it. Her chant was pure and painful across the clean air.

"Ahye-hanté, Ahye-hanté, naha-asti onyé!" The words pealed away, echoing up and down the space between the cliffs. As the last faded into those echoes, she leaned forward, her arms

spread like the wings of the swallows—or their son's feather cloak.

With the careless grace of a swallow, she soared from the cliff and down. She uttered no scream.

A shriek sounded in Uhtatse's heart, though his lips remained shut tightly. His eyes, at last, were able to close, and he stood in darkness for a long moment before he could force himself to move.

He turned to stare over the edge. She had vanished into the green growth of the Middle Way. Searchers surely could find her body, as they had not found her son's. He could guide them to her side, for he felt in himself the tearing of the tender leaves of the oak tree into which she plunged, the bruising of the grass that caught her at last.

His work remained to be done. He must not let the ending of his life as a man stop his work as the one who safeguarded his people. He must guard them for all that remained of his life . . .

But that life had shrunk to a very small space, indeed.

The world grew very cold, though it was still summer, and a very hot and dry one, too. Ahyallah, very old now, welcomed him to her house when he would come, and his sisters urged him to take his place before their fire pits and to dip his hands into their cook pots, yet he was in the grip of a depression that he could not shake away.

Every time he watched the swallows at their morning acrobatics, every time the quavering lilt of a flute shimmered in the air over the mesa, he thought of Ihyannah. When the sun sank in fires of red and gold or when he woke in the night to find no warm shape beside him, he thought of her and he wept for her.

Each child who piped a greeting to him as he moved about the mesa reminded him of his lost son, his lost wife. He missed Ki-shi-o-te acutely. The old man might have found a way to comfort him, though he would have been lost in his own grief as well. It was perhaps best that he went before his child.

Uhtatse felt that his spirit was scabbed over with grief, dulling its perceptions of the things that he must feel to do his work. He felt that he had aged many seasons in the brief span since Ihyannah's death, though he did his best to concentrate upon his work.

No bird flew or deer coughed that he did not note. Yet he found no hint of danger in all the land. He would have welcomed the threat of an attack . . . it would have reminded him that he was needed and revered among his people . . . and yet none came. The world was at peace, the weather for once unthreatening, and he was alone with his grief and loss. Even his life's work seemed unnecessary.

He went, at last, to his mother, though he did not find that easy to do. Not since he had married had he consulted his mother about the direction of his life.

She sat in her space in the three-dwelling complex in a medium-sized cave. Old as she was, her hands were busy at grinding corn in her worn metate, for her daughter's family shared the space with her, and she busied herself, as always, for their benefit. She nodded as he entered, and from time to time she glanced up at him as she worked.

Uhtatse knew that she sensed his need, but she was too wise to speak until he found words to offer. And at last those words came to him.

"The wind is cold, though it is early fall," he said while she poured meal into a tightly woven basket. "Though I am not yet ancient, I find my bones aching and my mind filled with dark things. My work does not warm me, and the sight of children laughing in the gardens with their mothers pains me to my heart.

"It is difficult for me to live, my mother."

From the warmth of her gaze, he understood that she had seen his need long before he admitted it to himself. She was a very old woman and a wise one, among a people whose women were strong and knowing. She set the basket into place and turned to sit again on her mat, facing him.

"You are caught at the hem of the past," she said. Her hands were again busy, twisting cordage and feeding into it the strips of rabbit fur that made the downy fiber from which the men wove blankets.

In the distance, there came the sound of drumming, and voices of men rose in an intricate chant from the direction of the nearest kiva. The corn festival was taking place, but he had not been able to force himself to attend the rituals.

"All that you loved was taken too suddenly," his mother said. "It did not give you time to prepare your spirit. You are living as a ghost, still fastened to that which was and unable to go forward, as yet, into that which will be." Her hands went still, and a line deepened between her brows.

"I know, for I, too, have lost those I loved. I, too, lived in perpetual twilight, seeing the sun only as a painful brightness that showed me all too clearly the things I did not wish to see. I thought of death, as did Ihyannah, yet I found a cure for that sickness of the spirit."

He watched her hands as they moved again, and his mind grew quiet under the spell of their rhythmic motions.

"What cure did you find?" he whispered. His eyes felt heavy, his hands and feet like lumps of wet clay that waited for the potter's hands.

"I went to the Old Woman Who Sings the Future. And she sang the future for me, though I had not believed that there could be one for her to sing to me. She proved me wrong. She sang of you and your sisters and of your Choosing. She sang about your sisters' children, who comfort my age.

"She showed me that there was always life, if I could climb around that terrible stone lying across my path. I wanted to think that my own grief meant that there would be no future for anyone . . . a silly thought for a woman almost grown, don't you think? Yet that is how you feel also, Uhtatse. It is what we all feel who lose those who hold our world in their hands."

Her own busy fingers spun the cordage, twirled fur into the twist, coiled it on a spindle. Uhtatse felt tensions he had not known he held inside himself begin to slip away. He knew he must do as his mother had done. The future was a terrible thing to know, and yet the Old Woman must sing his for him. He must learn again to live in the present as a functioning servant of his people.

A loop of gray hair slid from beneath Ahyallah's headband, and she pushed it back into place. Her lively black eyes searched her son's for some sign of understanding, and then she smiled.

With sudden clarity, Uhtatse was filled with a sense of his mother as a separate person, not simply as his mother. It was strange, for into his opened senses came the wild, free feel of a hawk quartering the sky. He understood that it was the shape of her spirit, and he had never known or even suspected that.

He nodded to her. "I will go to the Old Woman. I cannot continue as I have gone, and I am grateful, Ahyallah."

She said no more, though she smiled again, and her hands never slowed. Uhtatse turned and went away through her doorway and down the passage to find the steep pathway to the mesa.

XXXIII

He knew the way to the Old Woman's place as surely as he knew every inch of all the houses built into the cliffs. Down her precipitous pathway he went, into the big complex in which she had two rooms, an unthinkable luxury in the crowded places her people had built.

When he coughed outside her door, the Old Woman knew his cough, as she recognized every sound made by every one of her clan. "You may come, Uhtatse," she said, her voice high and thin with age. "Why does the One Who Smells the Wind come to my door? It is seldom that I speak with anyone now."

Uhtatse grunted as he bent to enter her door. He knew that she now spoke seldom with the Healer or the Teacher or himself. She had grown too ancient to waste her strength, and her own Mysteries, peculiar to the women, were now paramount in her mind. She did not need the lesser Man Arts for the sacred skills she used.

She had sung the future for his people since Ki-shi-o-te was a small boy. Her age counted so many seasons that the passing of more seemed to make no difference either in her age or herself. She held in her hands a most important part of the heritage of her people, and she was held in higher esteem than anyone else on the mesa, even those of other clans.

He felt humble, as her wise old eyes regarded him. A handful of grain that he had brought went into the bowl beside her, and with it he put a coil of juniper-bark cordage.

"I have come to ask you to sing the future. The past is gone, yet it clings to me. The present I cannot endure without some help. Only the future may cut me free of the thing that binds me. I ask it of you, who alone can sing the future."

She grinned, showing her toothless gums. "Oh, there is a young singer coming along," she muttered, taking the basket that lay beside her and shuffling over to empty the grain into another.

"When I die, it will not leave the People without any knowledge of what will come." She wound the cord tightly and put it, too, into her basket.

Uhtatse thought suddenly of a question that had troubled him for years. "Why do only women sing the future?" he asked. "And why is it that the old men sing only of the past?"

She laughed, a thin screech of merriment that cut through his mind like pain. "Women hold the future in their bellies; they look forward, always, keeping the young ones safe and seeing that they grow properly. We think of the men and women they will become and the children they will have, carrying our ways forward. Women must look to the future, for they have few trivial memories of hunting or of war to look back upon. Life is our business.

"The old men grow away from the present, always drawing deeper and deeper into the past. Their youth, their hunts and battles and contests obsess them. It is a simple thing, and you should have known without asking me." Her tone was querulous, and he felt that her rebuke was undeserved.

"I am only a man," he observed, his tone apologetic.

She seemed to accept the excuse, for she nodded. "But you want to know your future. I will sing it for you," she said.

"No!" he objected. "Not my own future. I want you to sing all of the future, as far as your gift will take you. I want to see this mesa in times so far distant that the Ahye-tum-datsehe, the Kiyate, and even the Tsununni are not even memories among men. Is that possible?"

Her faded eyes squinted up at him, staring deeply into his. Her face was as wrinkled as the runnels and the canyons that cut the lands about them. She had never had teeth since he could remember her. And yet an unquenchable strength lived in her gaze.

There was also fear. He could see it there, alongside the youth that had never quite been quenched in her spirit.

Something that she perceived in him seemed to reassure her. "It may be," she mused, "yes, it may be that you can bear it. It is possible that you might even understand it, though I have often tried, without success, to do that."

She grinned suddenly, turning her face into a map of creases. "So, the time has come when one of the People wants to look deeper into the seasons to come than merely his own life span. Wonderful! I had not thought that day would ever arrive. We will look together into that strange place that I sang for myself when I was younger and stronger and more curious." She gestured toward the mat on which she sat.

"Sit, and we will begin."

He folded himself onto the yucca matting and leaned against the sandstone wall as she muttered and fussed, settling herself comfortably on her blanket and folding her stiff legs into the same posture that Ki-shi-o-te had taught him as a boy.

She closed her eyes for a long moment, looking much like a corpse as she did so. When she opened them again, her mouth opened as well.

The chant, in ordinary people, was only music, better or worse as determined by the quality of their voices. But as Uhtatse listened to the Old Woman's song, he found himself caught into the quavering tones, and he saw with the inner vision now compelling her.

He saw himself sitting on a stone in the twilight, and he knew that he was as ancient in that vision as the Old Woman was in his present. Lights twinkled at him from the walls of the canyon, and he knew that the houses he had caused to be built into the cliffs were still secure, though there seemed to be many more than he knew.

He moved on a breeze through one of the almost-abandoned pueblos, and it was totally empty, its roof fallen away and its walls in ruins. Stones were tumbled about, and in places the wall stood no higher than his shoulder.

That breeze took him across the mesa. As he hung there, seasons shifted, and he saw snow deeper than any he had ever seen. Faster they shifted, and he realized that those deep snows were only there for a short span of years. Then the weather grew incredibly dry, by winter and by summer. He saw that there were no gardens showing green. There were, in fact, no runnels and no catchments to water any plantings there. Too dry to sustain their crops, no matter how well tended ... He sighed. That meant that his people must leave their ancient home and find another with a more kindly climate.

Then, for a very long time, there was nothing

on the mesa except the wind and the snow, the budding of the oaks in the Middle Way, the deer and the small animals, the hawks and the eagles and the magpies. In time, there came a few animals he did not know, and by that he realized that a very long time, indeed, must have passed.

Turkeys still gabbled about, scratching for food, but there were no people to be troubled by their noise and their dust. The wind swept past, on and on as he moved into the future.

And then there were men in the Middle Way, strange men, hairy and dressed in clothing unlike any that he knew. They sat atop huge beasts with hair growing from their necks and their tails in long whisks. The men stared about them as they made their way farther and farther into the land of the Ahye-tum-datsehe. He could see the astonishment on their faces as they stared up at the dwellings of his people, there in the cliffs.

Time spun past. A wide pathway opened, winding up the mesa in loops from the lowland at its foot. The great cliff still thrust its head against the sky, but everything else was changed. Shining things—animals? he thought not—sped up that new path, and in the juniper forest were people who were not like his own or any other people he knew. They held unidentifiable things in their hands; they walked about, talking an incomprehensible jargon, and he could not understand what they did or why, indeed, they were there at all.

The breeze rose again and carried his sensing into a building made of stone. It was not unlike a pueblo—and yet it was very different. On the walls were the things that his people made and used every day: to grind corn, to hold grain, to cook food.

There were many rooms there, and the breeze carried him slowly through them all, allowing him to see the things that his people had left behind them, now very faded and worn with time. He came to rest gently before a wall that was covered with something clearer than ice, yet as hard as stone.

Behind it was an old man, withered and dead and dried, as he had seen so many who had been located at the bottoms of crannies in the mesa, having lain there for years without being found. Beside the old man was a child, his face still showing the fear of his own death.

Ka-shay-neet! His son! These alien people had found him and had not sent him to the Other Place and the sun!

The child was dead, there could be no doubt. And yet he looked almost as if he might speak, as if he might greet his father across that terrible gorge of time and loss that parted them. There was no sign upon his body of the terrible fall he had sustained.

The strangers stood before that wall and looked up at his son, and their eyes seemed sad.

They seemed to feel for that child, who had died so young. He found it in his heart to think well of them, alien as they were . . . and then the breeze carried him forward. It became a wind, sweeping time before it as did Ahyallah's cornhusk broom.

The Old Woman's voice entered his mind again, now almost thinned to the whisper of a croak. The future dimmed. He could see nothing through the darkness that overtook the scene before him.

He opened his eyes in time to catch the Old Woman as she crumpled forward onto her blanket, though his inner vision was still filled with the wonder and terror of the things she had shown him.

"Ha-shay-ah!" said a voice behind him. Uhtatse turned, startled, to see who was there in the dark corner, but it was only a parrot, old and scraggly. It sidled forward to stand beside the fire pit and stare at the Old Woman.

Uhtatse laid her in a comfortable position and held a cup of water to her lips. She sipped stingily. Then her eyes opened, and she croaked, "Tso is the only one alive who uses my name. Everyone else is dead.

"It is good, sometimes, to be someone other than Old Woman." Her eyes closed, and she sighed gently.

The eyes opened once more. "They wondered why I lived for so long. But it was only to wait until I could show someone that future you have seen. Now that is done, and you can make of it what you want. I have done my work at last."

The words were little more than another sigh, and they went from her mouth on her last breath.

Uhtatse stood looking down at the withered shape, hardly larger than a child, that lay before the fire pit. The parrot stared and croaked *"Ha-shay-ah! Ha-shay-ah!"* again and again, as if it might call her back to life.

A woman came from the other room and stood silently, waiting for him to leave. She said nothing, and he nodded to her as he turned. This must be the new Woman Who Sang the Future, not yet old.

He wondered if she would be shown the marvels that he and Ha-shay-ah had seen. He hoped not, for that was not a comfortable future, into which they had looked together.

As he moved into the clean air of the mesa, he found himself thinking of something so strange, so impossible that it troubled his heart. He would, in some way, at some time, find a way to send his son's spirit to the Other Place. To take his body from that wall and give it the release of the ceremony of the sun.

XXXIV

Though the vision he had seen when the Old Woman died did not exactly comfort Uhtatse, it provided, if nothing else, much to think about. Where had those distant, alien people found the body of his son? Why was it, along with that of the old man, hung upon the wall of that building?

That future was bewildering to him, though he mulled over the things he had seen as he walked about the mesa at his work. A part of his mind seemed to shut itself away from his sensings and testings of the wind in order to think over the matters Ha-shay-ah had shown to him. The younger woman, who now sang the future, would not speak of the thing he had seen. She had not visited that distant place, and she had no wish to.

The year wore on into autumn, and he found the small house in the cliff too lonely and cold for one to live in. He moved into a middle-sized complex with a tall square tower, allowing a young couple to take Ihyannah's house for their dwelling. It comforted him a bit to think of them there together, as he and his wife had been.

Na-to-si and Karenni were still like brothers, but they had their own work and their growing families to think of. There was no time for them to go with him about his business on the mesa, and he found himself listening for the sound of small bare feet pattering through the dried grass. It was too painful to bear every time he realized that his son would never gaze with him from the high places, sense the hawks and the swallows, feel the living creatures walking about their lives.

He shut away his thoughts after a time, when he knew that he would never unravel the riddle of that future he had seen. Using every bit of his energy, he sent his senses across the distances, not because he expected any attack or even a visit of the Anensi so late in the year, but because he could not bear to keep his thought within the prison of his skull.

So it was that he felt the coming of a man. One single man. Down the canyon to the southeast came a tingle of life as the stranger moved there. With a less acute sensing, Uhtatse would never have known him to be there at all, yet the urgency of his pain had caused him to feel the coming of one who walked with a pain to rival his own.

He turned swiftly toward the meeting place

and called for the watcher there as he neared it in the first edge of twilight. Ha-no-na-say was making his way toward his own downward path from his counseling with the other elders as they made baskets, and he paused to wait for the One Who Smelled the Wind to come up to him.

"One comes," said Uhtatse. "A person, still very far away. He may come near in two suns' time, for he moves toward our mesa."

"An enemy?" The tone was sharp, for Ha-no-na-say had not forgotten the deaths that this man could have prevented.

"I think not. A man in pain, though not physically, as Karenni was. A man so filled with anger and grief that he is like one who goes mad in the sun. Yet there is something within him that I think is of value to us. He may bring word of the Tsununni. . . . The Anensi, in their last visit, had no idea where they hunted this year."

"Then tomorrow we will send one to meet this traveler and together we will see what it is that brings him to us," the Shaman said. He looked down the difficult stair to his home and sighed. "As I grow old, I find the way to my woman's house becoming more difficult, Uhtatse. I would have preferred a safe place for our homes that was easier to reach."

He set his foot properly into the first cranny and began his downward climb as Uhtatse watched. Suddenly he realized that Ha-no-na-say was now about the age that Ki-shi-o-te had been when he taught the young One Who

Smelled the Wind. The seasons rushed past, and he felt himself older by far than he had been a single season ago.

He must not leave the mesa to greet this newcomer, he knew. There was no reason to roam the countryside at this time of year. Where could he go to find something to distract his mind from his loneliness?

Then he thought of the Old Man Who Dreamed the Past. He was older by far, and who knew how many seasons might be left to him? To balance that glimpse of the future, why should he not see a vision of the past? That would leave him, like an insect caught in a spiderweb, suspended between the two, and yet he felt strangely comfortable with the thought.

The way to the path leading down into the tiny house shared by the Old Man and his equally old woman was long, and the stars were staring down as Uhtatse tapped on the stone lip of the cliff to warn the pair of his visit. After a time there came a tiny clicking from below, and he smiled and moved down, feeling his way effortlessly.

Koo-tah-hi stood in his doorway, silhouetted against the glimmer from his fire pit. "You are welcome here," he said formally, as if he knew that this was no ordinary visit. "Come into Haliya's house and share our daily meal."

That reminded Uhtatse that he had not eaten that day. The day before? He could not remember, and that made him think of Ihyannah's insistence that he eat well before going out on the mesa. Old ones like these did not use up so much energy, and one meal a day was enough for them.

He ducked his head to enter the house and smiled at Haliya, who crouched over a pot, dropping in a hot stone that stirred good smells of corn and beans and squash in its depths. He found that he was very hungry, and he accepted a bowl of food gratefully when it was ready.

When they had eaten and talked enough to satisfy politeness, he turned to Koo-tah-hi. "I would like for you to sing the past for me," he said. "The Old Woman gave me the future and died. I would like to know the vision that you see while you are young enough to have the strength for singing it."

Koo-tah-hi did not look surprised . . . that was a thing he never did. His eyebrow twitched minutely, and he stared into the fire.

"It is long since any of the Ahye-tum-datsehe have asked for my vision," he said. "I had thought that I might go into the Other Place without ever visiting it again. I am glad that you have come."

Without any preparation, he leaned back against the wall of the house and closed his eyes. Uhtatse, sitting on the bench against the opposite wall with the fire pit between them, leaned back, too, but he did not yet close his eyes. He watched as the old man concentrated, seeming to grow even more wrinkled and frail as he did so.

His chant was thin, but it sounded loud in the small space. The syllables grew in intensity, and Uhtatse began to see the thing that formed in the old one's mind.

Water . . . he saw more water than he had ever dreamed might exist, even after hearing Ra-onto's tales about the Great Waters to the east and west. Waves like the ripples on the catchment basins, magnified hugely, rolled across the inside of his mind, crashing against cliffs, wearing away holes in the softer stone . . . the vision faded.

People were on the mesa. He recognized the spot where he often lay and gazed out over the lower canyon lands. They did not wear the sorts of cloaks he knew, being almost naked, though there was snow on the ground about their feet. They were gesturing to each other, their hands flying, their faces showing excitement.

The vision shifted, and he saw hunters, using the atlatl, downing a deer and carrying it away on a pole. He followed them as they neared the highest ridge of the mesa, where they came into a cleared space where fires burned. About that space there were pit houses . . . and he knew suddenly that the big pueblo should stand there. There was no sign of it, only the humble little dugout homes that had all but been abandoned when he was a boy.

The chant changed its rhythm. About that

place there grew up small stone houses, scattered about the area. Even as he watched, they
were torn down, their blocks being used to con-
struct a pueblo that he realized had grown, over
the generations, into the one he knew.

As it had before, time began whipping past
with terrible speed. He saw people like the
Ahye-tum-datsehe as they built up the catchments, cleared the runnels, and learned to
make their beautiful decorated pottery and
weave their fur and feather blankets.

From time to time there came a quick
glimpse of the Anensi, or a swift battle with the
Kiyate, and he knew they neared his own time.
How many seasons had the old man sung while
the stars wheeled overhead and the old woman
put fresh bits of wood into the fire pit?

The chant came to a quavering end, and Koo-
tah-hi opened his eyes. "When I was younger, it
was longer. It seems that I lack the energy for
the great visions I used to see. But you saw . . .
I felt you as you saw it with me."

"Yes," said Uhtatse. "I saw. And I am grateful, Old One, for your vision. Perhaps this will
help me to do my work and live my life, as the
Old Woman's vision has not."

The old man shook his head, his gray strag-
gle of hair moving against his shoulders. "No
chant, no word, no person can help you with
that. It is a thing that only time can heal. I have
seen it often. Indeed, I lost my first family when
the fever came, years before you were born.

This woman came to me after I had learned to let time flow over me without allowing myself to grieve."

She smiled and put a large chunk onto the fire. Her gapped teeth were dark in the firelight, her face furrowed, her eyes dimmed with age, but Uhtatse knew that to Koo-tah-hi she was beautiful, as Ihyannah would have been to him, no matter how old they grew together.

He shook aside the thought and took his leave of the pair. He found it in him to be glad that they still had each other, even though he had no one.

As he walked through the chilly fall night toward his own place, someone came to greet him. It was his sister's son, In-teh-ka, waiting for his return. His heart warmed a bit from its frozen state as the boy put a small hand up to find his.

"Uncle, I have learned to weave. Come and see!" the young voice piped.

Uhtatse squeezed the little fingers gently and turned with the child to their own downward path. He was not totally alone as long as his sisters had children. That empty space in his heart would heal. At last he knew that, for something in that long tale of life on his mesa had told him that men went forward with their lives, never back.

He would live and do his work. And in time he might even find his heart thawed in his forlorn breast.

XXXV

A moon grew into roundness and began to dwindle. The man he had felt approaching drew nearer to the mesa, and the burden of grief and fury he carried almost overrode the other perceptions that should have occupied Uhtatse's mind while the business of the People went upon its way and the crops began to be harvested and dried or stored in pots against the winter.

At last he could endure it no more and went to Ha-no-na-say. "We must send a runner to guide that man to our mesa. There is something within his mind and spirit that grips me, and it can only be because it has to do with the welfare of our people. Send Mo-tu-o, who is young and swift, so that I may once again do my duty as the One Who Smells the Wind."

The man stared into his eyes as if assessing his need. What he read there told him much, and he nodded. "Mo-tu-o will go now," he said.

The young man, indeed, was glad of the chance to be away from his regular work, running down the wind toward the newcomer. It had been a long while since the Anensi last visited them, and they were hungry for news of others who lived in the lands about them.

When Mo-tu-o had gone, Uhtatse felt a great relief of spirit. He was able once again to range his territory, feeling the creatures that were his responsibility, assessing the wind and the cloud, the soil and the sky. And yet a part of his thought traveled with the youth across the lands he had roamed with Ihyannah and even beyond.

He knew when the two met down in the forested mountains to the south and east, and he knew when they turned their steps toward the mesa. That gave him a more peaceful spirit than he had possessed in a long while as he waited for them to come.

At last they were on the very soil of his home, and he moved toward the path where the guardian watched. As the pair paused to give the signal below and the guardian called a welcome, he tensed, wondering what link had pulled him so tightly to this stranger.

And then he understood, in a flash of fire-bright comprehension, that this was not a stranger at all. He knew this man, though he had not seen him since they were boys. Ra-onto had come with the Anensi when he had been a lad in training. Other groups of the Anensi had visited the mesa in the years since, though his had not, but there could be no mistaking the erect stance, the proud lift of the head, though it was now becoming gray.

Uhtatse stepped forward to greet his old friend, and Ra-onto, looking upward, saw him and almost checked his steps. He, too, knew.

"Uhtatse," he said, his tone firm but filled with some haunting emotion that chilled the listener to the bone.

They gazed, eye into eye, for a moment before the newcomers reached the level ground and all three set off for the complex occupied by Uhtatse's people. The guardian resumed his watch behind them, but the One Who Smelled the Wind felt a chill of unease as he felt those long spans of countryside lying about the mesa.

Ka-hiya, the shaman of the West Mesa people, stood on an outcrop, watching them, and Uhtatse raised his hand in reassurance. He knew that his counterparts, all along the split mesa, would have felt this stranger's arrival. He knew also that they would wait until tomorrow to come to learn what news he brought with him from the world outside.

Even with Ra-onto walking beside him, Uhtatse felt a strange unease. There was more to this meeting than boys meeting again as old men. The pain he had felt across the miles was something that would affect his own kind, he was certain. He found himself wondering where might be the clan of Anensi who had been this man's people. They had been a tight-knit group, well able to care for their own.

As if feeling his thought, Ra-onto turned to look into his face, and deep in his eyes lived a tale that Uhtatse felt a terrible reluctance to hear. Or to live . . . and with that thought came the knowledge of what must be done.

They reached the great house on the promontory, which was used for meetings of the different clans living on the mesa. Its large kiva was big enough for all the men who would or could come, and he knew that groups would even now be readying themselves to travel there tomorrow. The others who sensed the mesa were almost as skillful as he, and they would understand that something important and unsettling had come among them.

When Ra-onto came into the small chamber Uhtatse shared with his nephew, as the guest of the house, he looked about and smiled, though the widening of his lips seemed more like a grimace of agony.

"Your people have planned well. They will survive here, while others fall beneath the weight of those who destroyed my own kind."

"Say nothing now," Uhtatse said. "Tomorrow, when you are rested and fed, we will go into the kiva and you may tell all the men what you have seen. Tonight we will only talk of unimportant matters and sleep dreamlessly, for I dread tomorrow, and I feel that you do as well." He gestured toward a bench along one wall of the room. "You may use that side. In-teh-ka and I sleep head to head, so that we may talk in the night without disturbing the others in my sister's house."

"I had a nephew. I had a daughter who was swift as the wind and bright as an autumn leaf. I had two wives, who knew far more than they ever told."

The grief in Ra-onto's voice made Uhtatse's skin ridge into gooseflesh. "Tomorrow," he said again. "Tomorrow."

He brought a pot of cooked food and they ate together, without words. The only thought in the Anensi's mind was of his own trouble, and as Uhtatse refused to hear it twice, it was best so.

When they slept at last, Uhtatse found that he dreamed, after all, and quick glimpses of dark images struggling, faces twisted with rage and terror, haunted his night.

He rose in the dimness before dawn to join his old acquaintance, who sat on the bench staring into nothingness; he found that he was impatient for the experience in the kiva. That, perhaps, would end this borrowed misery.

And yet he had the feeling that, instead, it might introduce unhappiness far worse than any his people had known before now.

XXXVI

In the morning, as Uhtatse had known, the meeting place was filled with those who came to hear the words of the newcomer. From the West Mesa, from the other clans of the East Mesa, the Ahye-tum-datsehe converged, until there was no room in the kiva for all the men, and they crouched on its roof instead.

The women and children sat cross-legged around the edges, listening too, as Ra-onto and Uhtatse came onto the mesa and approached the waiting people. Ha-no-na-say was already there, and the new Woman Who Sang the Future sat beside him.

Uhtatse did not speak; that was, he always thought, the task of Ha-no-na-say when others came to speak with his clan. So the Teacher rose at last and welcomed the visitors to his Council House. And when he had finished, he gestured for Ra-onto to speak.

The man rose to his full height, straightening

his back, raising his head, letting the strong light of the new sun show the tracks of age and grief upon his face. His eyes held deep pain, and the Elders and the people shrank, almost invisibly, from the wash of agony that radiated from him.

"I have come across the lands alone," said Ra-onto. "Though I started from the southern country, with my people richly laden with trade goods meant for those in the northern countries, I have come here alone, the last and only survivor of all those Anensi of my family-clan."

Now there was a gentle hissing as everyone sighed together. Such a catastrophe was a thing they could hardly comprehend or believe.

As the man's voice began his account, Uh-tatse closed his eyes. His sensing, stronger now than it had ever been, penetrated the voice, the words, the man himself, taking part in the memories driving the words, as if he had been there.

The sun shone with an intensity that he had never known. The lines of Anensi, walking together, ordering the travois dogs, controlling the excursions of the children after butterflies or hop toads, raised a thin veil of dust beneath their heels, and it rasped in his throat.

The River was ahead, and there the clan that was heading eastward split off toward their own chosen territory for the year. Those who would go north angled away, too, when the time came, and he moved with the clan, said farewells to those who left it, and went forward with those heading for the mountain country.

The nights came, with warm breezes and the scents of flowers in time, as they reached softer climates, with more abundant waters. The People laughed and traded with the others living along the streams they crossed and, later, those following the Horned Ones as they moved in measureless tides over the grasslands.

And one night, when the clan had again traveled long over the dry country, there came a shrilling in the darkness. He rose, his pulses drumming with alarm, sleep suddenly shaken from his eyes and his mind.

"Take cover!" he shouted as he dashed between the bodies that were now beginning to move. "Where is the Battle Chief?"

There was scanty starlight, no moon, and the pale grasses gave no glimmer of light as he stumbled forward, his flint knife in his hand, his eyes seeking desperately for some enemy to attack. There was no reply to his shout, and when he came to the spot where the Battle Chief had rested between his wives, he understood. All three were dead.

His seeking hands found a warm stickiness as he felt the severed throats. Some bold enemy had slipped among the sleepers of the clan to find this warrior who might have led an effective resistance. And now his people were dying in the darkness, and there was nothing he could do.

Who would attack the trading people? What enemy was so rash and so uncaring that they would cut themselves off from the trade that tied the kinds of peoples together?

He turned back toward his own family's resting place, calling for his wives, his daughter, his sons and their families, but amid the tumult and the wails he could hear no answer.

He struck out at a swift body passing by, whose alien scent told him it was not one of his own. There was a gasp, something struck his head, and the night dissolved into nothingness.

Uhtatse came back into himself suddenly, to find that Ra-onto had paused for a moment. As he blinked his eyes, the voice went on, " . . . and in the morning, I found that my part of the clan had been cut by half. One of my wives was slaughtered in her blood, the other wounded, and my daughter was not to be found, dead or living.

"We huddled together, there on the plain, and there was nothing to be seen in any direction. No enemy. No corpses of our missing ones. Only our own dead surrounded us, and we had no fuel in sufficient quantities for burning them in order to send their spirits to the Other Place. So we buried them in the shallow soil and set what stones we could find over the mound containing their bodies."

"But still you had many people," said Ha-no-na-say. "And you had warning. Surely you could have found a way to thwart that enemy!"

"So we thought," the man replied, his head bowed now, his back less straight. "But it was not so.

"They struck us at midday, rising as if by witchcraft from the dust at our feet to strike down those nearest them. We fought, now that we could see, but their fury was terrible and irresistible, and more of us were lost.

"We built fires, that night, of the dried dung of the Horned Ones, and half of us watched while the rest slept. And when the sun rose, of those who had slept half did not rise to greet it, for they had been slain by ones who could creep, unseen, even in the lights of our fires, even past the eyes of our watchers. My second wife did not rise on that morning."

Uhtatse felt the old pain rise into his throat. If he had suffered the loss of one wife with such agony, what had Ra-onto felt at losing two?

"We went forward. What was behind us, save the bodies of our dead? We still had trade goods, but now we did not value them as we had done, for we all felt that we would never survive to give them into the hands of those who waited for them, or to take, in turn, those things they would trade. But we are—or we were—traders. That is all we knew. We followed our route toward the people who live in the mountains, and eventually toward this mesa.

"When the world has gone mad and everything is lost or broken, it seems that a man must follow his habits still, or lie down and die for lack of purpose."

Ha-no-na-say filled the pause in his words with a wordless chant, sad and faint and filled with a strange feeling of foreboding. Uhtatse felt his heart echo the sounds as Ra-onto pulled his thoughts out of his inner self and began to speak again.

"They attacked at dawn and at dusk, at midnight and at noon. We never knew when or where—or from what dust devil or idle breeze they would appear. They cut us down from four double hands to two in one night. From that number to two single hands, to one, to four individuals, then to two.

"At that point, they seemed to lose interest in us, and See-chevo and I thought for a time that we might be left unmolested as we hurried toward the distant mountains, where there might be cover, a hiding place of some sort in which we could shelter from those demons.

"We left our trade goods strewn in the plains, and I think that those who killed us did not even care to steal them. They seemed to want only blood and death, and that we gave them in plenty. Yet, though we killed many of their number, there seemed always to be more.

"On the day we reached the foothills, finding a stream amid fir trees, they struck for the last time. See-chevo went down with an arrow in his eye, shot from cover, so that I could not see who killed him. They left me standing alone, wanting death, begging them to take me along with all of my people.

"But they are more than cruel. They would not give me death, and so I came to you to warn you of their coming."

"But they are not here," objected Ha-no-na-say. "Surely they could have traveled here as quickly as you."

"They have not traveled the mountains and the plains for the many lives of men that my people have," said the trader. "They do not know the fast trails, the hidden passes, the tiny water holes that cannot be found if you do not know where to look. No one can travel as quickly as the Anensi when there is need. I know they will come here. I felt them behind me as I moved.

"Leaders of the Ahye-tum-datsehe, be warned. The Tsununni will come soon."

There was a long silence, broken only by the wail of a feverish infant and the distant gabble of the turkeys. Uhtatse found himself cold with an inner chill he had not known before, even when the Tsununni attacked for the first time. The losses on the mesa had been few, and yet no life could be spared that might be saved. The agonies of the Tsununni who paid with pain for the misdeeds of their kind still came to him sometimes in dreams, and he would wake sweating and go onto the mesa to walk away the memory.

They had known that another attack would come. The Kiyate had paid visit after visit to their stronghold ... why should this new warrior kind not do the same? And yet he had hoped that his sisters' children might never smell hot blood spilled on sunlit stone, the smoke of burning bodies, or the acrid scent of fear among many people. He had known, even as he hoped, that this was an impossible dream, and yet it had remained with him, comforting his loneliness.

Now it was time, once more, to string bows afresh, to make baskets of arrows, to sharpen short spears and gather stones for slings. And this time, the war they would fight would be totally new, for this would be the first they waged from the security of their homes in the cliff caverns. They must talk together, think long, and invent new methods for protecting their fields, their neighbors, and their mesa-top people from the ferocity of the Tsununni.

XXXVII

The summer was a dry one, as many seemed to be then, with terrific heat even high on their mesa. They could not find it in them to plan the use of fire, no matter what happened, for the juniper and the piñon were tinder dry, waiting for a spark of any sort to set off a blaze that might well clear the entire area of growth. The small fires, caused at times by lightning or an escaped spark from a cook fire, were matters for grave concern, requiring every available hand for fighting them down. A deliberate conflagration was unthinkable, even now. Without the trees, their lives would have been all but impossible.

As the people drifted away from the meeting place, their faces still with worry, their words quiet and intense, Uhtatse looked off across the canyon beyond the place where they had all met. The Tsununni might, once again, move up from the Middle Way, climbing the cliffs. If they used the indentations his people had chipped for their own uses, they would find, on arriving at the top, that one who did not know how to begin that climb could not complete it—and if others came behind? He almost chuckled at the thought.

The old and the ill, the children and the pregnant women would be safe in the houses in the cliffs, of course, but all the rest must put their minds to inventing a way to safeguard their gardens, which were skimpy enough because of the drought. Every effort had been made to water them from the dwindling catchments, and it would be a hungry winter, even if all went well for the rest of the year.

But if the Tsununni trampled or burned the food plants, some would surely starve. Uhtatse turned to his nephew, who, as usual, was at his heels. "We must get the women to go through the gardens and pick everything that will ripen in storage. Everything! Go and tell your mother."

In-teh-ka looked up at him, his small face frowning with concentration as he absorbed the command. Uhtatse knew that the boy's quick mind had already grasped the meaning of that message that was, even now, accompanying his swift feet surely along the broken ground to the spot where his mother and his father were talking together.

Again, Uhtatse went to the promontory that had taught him so much over the years of his

life. It was vital that he learn where the Tsununni were, how long it might be before they
followed their victim here. His skills were not
sufficient to read their presence surely over the
distance that separated them from him . . . only
his old friendship with Ra-onto had allowed
him to feel his approach, and there was no such
bond between any of the Ahye-tum-datsehe and
the Tsununni.

He sighed as he began the dangerous descent. His limbs were not as young as they had
been; his fingers and toes were already crook-
ing with the arthritis that was the bane of his
people. Pain accompanied every inch of his
climb to the niche that awaited him. But pain
was good . . . it made the spirit tender, recep-
tive, and ready to know and understand things
that it might miss entirely otherwise.

He stood in the narrow space, his eyes open
and yet unseeing, for he was feeling outward
with his sensing, past the mesa, past the Middle Way, past the canyons and the wooded hills
and mountains to the east. The small lives he
touched he disregarded. They belonged where
they were, going about their business of living.
No, he must go farther and farther still—to the
edges of the world, if necessary—to find the
enemy of his people.

But it was too soon, and he knew it. Only
fasting and pain and the peeling away of the
layers of self, one by one, in the dry heat and

thirst and intensity of effort and time, could make that happen. He closed his eyes at last and breathed deeply, willing his body and his spirit to do the thing he demanded of them.

Time, as usual, slid past imperceptibly, for he was locked once again in battle with himself and his circumstances. The other efforts he had made here had seemed to take everything he had, more effort than he had known he possessed, more will and endurance than he could find. And yet he had made them, and they had served him well.

Now he knew that those were the feeble steps of an infant, compared with the stringent journey he now must make through his will and his spirit before he could fly free above those distant heights to find what he was seeking. Age brings pain and a longing for ease, but he discarded that thought and kept himself still and silent as day and night slid over him, leaving him, each time, more sensitive to everything occurring on the mesa.

The pain in his knees and shoulders became intense, but he pushed it away from his mind, down into that place where such unimportant matters must wait until the time becomes right to attend to them. His breath rasped harshly through his dry throat, and his chest began to hurt as well. He was old, some buried instinct told him. Too old to compel his flesh so stubbornly. That thought, too, he thrust away into the well of self that he had sealed from his consciousness.

Still time passed, though he had lost any thought of that. His skin was weathering, his mouth was like stone or juniper bark, and his eyeballs dried to the point at which the act of shifting his gaze was torment.

On the day when his tough and yet aging body was almost ready to fall, leaving his spirit to wander free forever, something inside him seemed to split like a dried seed pod, and a self he had not known was within him came drifting upward, away from that body, out over the canyon without any threat of falling.

Uhtatse looked down with astonishment to see a dark and withered shape stuck into the niche where he had stood for so long. He still went upward, until he could stare over the entire mesa, even to the other part of the divided eminence. The villages of the other Ahye-tumdatsehe, abandoned now for the most part, showed as huddles of squared stone against the pale soil and rock.

Now he was high above his home, turning gently as if in a warm breeze, setting this face, which he suspected was far different from that old one down there, toward the east and the south. Below and behind him trailed a filament that seemed to connect him still to his distant flesh, but it was no hindrance and he ignored it. Mountains slid past below him, more rapidly than a man could run or even an eagle could fly, he thought. Rifts in the earth, tall peaks, forests of trees so large that they hardly seemed the same sort as his familiar junipers and piñons passed beneath him.

And then something inside this strange new body sprang to attention. There was life below—not animals, not the other clans of humankind who wandered the high country, but hatefully familiar. The sparks of living beings seemed to draw him downward toward the forests, which were turning yellow from the heat and the drought.

He could see, as he descended, cuts where streams had polished stones round and smooth, and where now only small trickles of water ran. Beside such a stream there was a camp, where women and children moved about the business of skinning game, trapping hares, gathering seeds and roots from the forest.

The men ... where were the men? He dropped lower still, his sensing acute. And he found them, squatting on their heels in a shadowy spot, their hands busy with weapons, sharpening flint knives, smoothing scarred arrow shafts, shaping arrowheads from obsidian shattered from the mountain walls about them. Always readying for war were the Tsununni, he guessed.

This was a small band ... too small for the work they had done upon the Anensi. They were evidently a part of a clan of barbarians

who did not understand that one never attacked the traders who supplied all the peoples
of all the lands with the things they could not
make for themselves. Uhtatse felt sick, for
these looked like human beings. They talked
together peaceably, as did his own kind.

And yet they, with other groups that must be
scattered along the long road behind them,
were a desperate threat to his own kind. And
how long would it be before they came to the
country of the Ahye-tum-datsehe? It was impossible to judge as he traveled.

He knew with sudden certainty that this was
the nearest of the bands to his own place. If he
went very low, very slowly, toward the setting
sun, he might determine how many hands of
days would bring them to the mesa.

He dropped to the springy soil beneath one of
the huge firs below him, very near the group of
men. He knew they would not see him—he
could hardly see his own hand, which glim-
mered like cobweb before his eyes. These barbarians could never perceive such a gossamer
presence among them. He stalked through the
middle of the group and headed away, recalling
with sure accuracy the direction in which he
must go.

In such country, he found very quickly, one
must follow a stream. That showed unerringly
the easiest route over the peaks that ringed
him on every hand. And so he went away up-
stream, his feet not quite touching the stony

soil as he made the motions of walking homeward.

When darkness fell, he walked still, finding that this not-body did not tire or hunger or thirst. He wondered with sudden interest how that old twig of a body fared back in the niche where it waited, but that seemed a very minor consideration. To go back into that painful flesh was not a thing he looked forward to doing, no matter what the need might be.

Night and day he walked, knowing that those who followed behind would not be able to travel so constantly. Yet he measured the time required for his journey as he moved through the tumbled peaks, past the quiet forests that sighed with wind through needled branches, beside bears fishing in the shallow remnant of the stream or wolves pacing secretly through the night over the distance he had come. He knew that he could tell within a matter of hours how long it would take the Tsununni to come, once again, to the home of his people.

When he came into familiar ways, whose distance was known to him, he took to the air again, soaring higher even than the eagles he knew of old, passing them as they circled upon the swirling air, feeling their astonishment as they sensed a presence they could not see. He spent a tiny fragment of his time in feeling out the freedom of the sky, and when he turned toward the mesa and the waiting niche he felt a chill of loss. And yet he knew that he must go back, put on that ragged garment, all but worn out as it was, and give his people the news he carried.

They would have a moon, or slightly less, in which to form their battle plans, secure their supplies, and organize the clans of the mesa for war. It was less than he would have liked, but it was also longer than it might have been.

As he drifted downward, slipped into the dried husk he had left behind him, felt again the pain and the thirst, he knew that he would long for the rest of his days for the freedom and the delight of that journey he had made. He wondered if that was the way in which one traveled into the Other Place . . . . If that were true, he might be the only man ever to go there and to come again to his life.

And then he was solidly inside himself, feeling the agony in his bones and muscles, the dwindling spark that was his life. And he found as well that there was no strength left in him to make the climb back to the mesa top.

Would his efforts be wasted after all? That seemed a terrible thing. He forced his hands to move, his legs, his head to turn upon his neck, trying to loosen the stiff muscles. He leaned from the niche . . . and almost fell.

For the first time in all his life, he knew that he must have help to do the things he still had to accomplish. Had his nephew stood guard above him after delivering the message he had sent? The boy often did such things.

"In-teh-ka!" he called, his voice a hoarse croak hardly audible even to himself. "In-teh-ka!"

From high above there came a tumble of gravels. A small voice shrilled, "My uncle! Are you all right?"

Uhtatse smiled. He would survive now, to give his news to the People.

XXXVIII

The old man on the mesa shivered in the wind, which was now sharp and chill. He could still feel in his ancient body the echo of that old pain as he made his way back to speak to his people. But he could also feel a remnant of the joy of that flight among the eagles.

He sat in the starlight, the uneven edges of his cloak flipping against his ankles and about his shoulders, as he stared up into the vast darkness above him. He wondered yet again about the lights hanging there, seeming so near that he might reach to touch them and yet so distant that not even an echo rang from their starry shapes. His life had been spent in wondering about such matters, even as he sensed his surroundings, keeping watch over the Ahye-tum-datsehe.

Now that the responsibility was no longer his, he found himself filled with all the questions his long life had brought to him. It seemed that he had forgotten none of them, as though they had been packed away in some invisible storage jar of his mind. Now he brought them forth again and measured them against the things he had learned, painfully and with terrible effort, over the seasons that tallied his age.

Below, the fires had dwindled, and little light marked the homes of his people in the cliff. That was one of the things he had learned, he mused. You can warn people. You can show them the ways that will safeguard them. And yet no warning, no reasoning, no showing will affect them until they have seen the face of disaster and suffered catastrophe.

"You cannot make people safe. No, you cannot force them to do the right and reasonable thing, no matter how important it may be. It was only the first attack of the Tsununni that allowed us to be ready for that terrible one." His reedy voice was hardly louder than the wind across the rocks, but he felt that it understood his words. The wind had been shaking people into awareness for much longer than he had done.

He huddled his shoulders deeper into his cloak, feeling the cold now inside his bones and his blood, creeping slowly toward his heart. It would not be long now. He would, perhaps, find the answers to all those questions at last, before the night was done.

But he had come to the place of that battle, and he found that his mind would not relinquish the memory. He must live, still again, *that time of blood and anger and death, once more impotent to affect the fighting or the outcome.*

He remembered the sharpness of the rocks among which he had sheltered, keeping his hands free of blood so that he might, in the future, warn his people as he had done this time. That was more important to them than any death he might cause with a club or an arrow or a spear.

He had not been able, however, to turn off his overacute sensing. He had lived the battle in which he had not been able to participate.

△△

XXXIX

▽▽

The heat and drought had been drying up the streams, searing the grasses and the trees, killing even the youngest of the tough yucca plants for weeks. The approach of the Tsununni was not made easier by the discomfort caused by the elements, and the Ahye-tum-datsehe went about their preparations with desperate yet sluggish haste.

Even as they worked, Uhtatse was going about his normal course, walking the mesa from end to end, going down into the Middle Way and even out onto the low country below it, feeling for the unease of the animals in the countryside through which the enemy would come. There was nothing as yet from that quarter, but he tingled with something anticipatory. His nerves felt raw, his nose kept turning up as he smelled the dusty air.

He went back up onto the mesa early and sat on the stone upon which he had found the mutilated watchers when the enemy first came. He faced north and west, for there was a disturbance there. Weather. He had been expecting something of the sort, for such a period of terrible stress was usually relieved by an equally terrible storm. And from the feel of his bones and his twinging, arthritic joints, this was going to be a bad one.

He found his way back to his part of the high ground and sought out Ha-no-na-say. "There is a storm three days away. Watch the clouds, my old friend. We may have to keep our enemies at bay in the midst of wind and rain."

The Shaman looked up, following Uhtatse's gaze toward the north. Fine wisps of cloud hung almost out of sight at the edge of the sky. He sighed and nodded. "It is so."

That warning made the women work faster in the gardens, for such a storm would devastate much of the foodstuff there. The corn was not yet ripe, it was true, and it would mold if harvested so young, but they staked the plants in order to keep them from being swept flat into the earth, and they regretfully cut the small, tender squash into rounds for drying. Little was better than nothing, as they had found over the generations of their life on the mesa.

On the morning of the second day, moving on his round, Uhtatse felt the first flicker of the enemy's approach, which was reflected in the sensing of the animals below. That sent him back among his people, giving them time limits

for their work. All who were going into the cliffsides must be there long before the Tsununni
came within range of their homes. All the rest
must get into position and remain there, still
and silent, no matter how weary and discouraged they might become.

The Tsununni must not suspect that this isolated people on the high ground expected their
coming. The youngsters who were old enough to
playact were assigned to continue their games
in the dust outside the pueblos, and some of the
older people sat against the walls, seeming to
doze or to weave or spin yucca fiber. There were
enough people visible to make the abandoned
Big House seem to be a normally tenanted village.

As the third day dawned, all were ready,
though Uhtatse knew that it would be late before the enemy came into position to begin
climbing onto the mesa. Every person of his
clan, and those in the others up and down the
joined mesas, had a task to perform, if only that
of remaining quiet and out of sight while the
day went forward. Everyone, he hoped, was in
place and ready to take part in the defense of all
their homes.

The sky, as he was uneasily aware, was
threatening, and no sun rose over the eastern
canyon rim. Purple clouds lay across the northwest, and the breeze sighed nervously over the
junipers and piñons, whispering among their

needles and flicking pinches of dust into the noses and eyes of those who waited.

Uhtatse was concealed in a cranny on the cliffside, watching, listening, feeling, smelling the pregnant air, which was tanged with the scents of alien bodies as well as with the distant smell of rain. The Middle Way was already disturbed by the passage of the Tsununni. He could feel deer fleeing away from them, bounding over clumps of serviceberry, darting between stands of small oaks.

The eagles, tumbling in the upper air currents, were paying attention only to their own flying, not to the building tension below them, and he knew they would soon seek their aeries to shelter from the storm. He could feel, almost as a physical pain, a point of intolerable pressure out on the plains to the northwest, and he knew that one of the devil-winds must be whirling the lands to destruction beyond the horizon.

And then the Tsununni began their long climbs, a small group here, an individual there, a larger party upon a more promising route upward. They were, he decided, not greatly skilled at such work, though they climbed well. They were not the equals of those who spent their lives clambering up and down the precipices, however, and he knew that they would arrive at the top both tired and shaken. Those routes they took were not easy ones, for there were no easy ones, and some he had damaged subtly, so as to send an unknowing climber back down faster than he had come.

He eeled away from the edge, through the stiff yucca and the wiry grass, to find one of the runnels that ran away in the right direction. He came to Ha-no-na-say's position with fair speed, to find the old Teacher all but invisible among the concealing junipers. He had his weapons at hand, the bow for long distance, the flint knife and the short spear for closer work. He had spent his youth learning such skills, as they all had, and any Tsununni who thought to find them unfit warriors was certain of disappointment.

"They are climbing now," he said softly. "The first will come to the top near the Meeting Place. Natosi is there, with a handful of warriors, and they will not, I think, be a problem for us here. But others will arrive soon. Send the runners to warn the attack groups."

One of the youngest of the men—little more than a boy, actually—set off, stooped behind the scanty growth, to take the word, and Uhtatse turned toward the spot from which he would endure this battle. His was, he thought bitterly, the most difficult of all the tasks appointed to his people.

He must feel what happened, no matter who lived and who died, without being able to lift a hand to change anything.

XL

The watchers came in from their posts, slipping silently ahead of the attackers, keeping sharp lookout for any who came up the mesa in unusual places. As Uhtatse settled into his task of sensing without taking part, he felt other clans in other parts of the twinned mesas also luring the Tsununni onward, pretending not to have kept watch at all.

He had no wish ever to find a lookout served as those others had been when the Tsununni first came up the cliffs, and he had consulted with the clans over the best way to preserve lives without sacrificing alertness. All had agreed that this was the best strategy, and he could feel the stealthy retreat of the People as the Tsununni crept near the cliff tops.

The wind was gusting now from the north and west, tossing the junipers, whistling through the needles of the piñons, dashing grit into the eyes of those who were moving up the steeps. Uhtatse could feel a sort of tension building inside him, as much from the weather as from the approaching battle, and he strove to remain calm, to feel and recall everything that happened.

When this was over, if he and his people still lived, he would tell it all to the Old Man Who Dreamed the Past. It would go into his history of the Ahye-tum-datsehe along with the account of everyone else who survived this confrontation.

But he put that out of his mind as he concentrated his senses upon the drama unfolding about his home. He felt the eagle, very high now, rolling on the gusts of wind. He felt the deer, disturbed by these intruders into the Middle Way, begin moving to distant places as more warriors began the climb to the top of the mesa.

Honing his perceptions to raw alertness, he felt for those men who were coming. They slipped through the scrubby oaks like shadows, their motions concealed by the whipping of the vegetation in the wind. They came to the cliff, a difficult climb in good weather and one that only very brave men would attempt.

A scout, he thought, moved back to direct the climbers toward a crevice that promised access to the top, and soon a line of warriors crept up the long chimney leading from the Middle Way to a point on the promontory beyond the Meeting Place.

Uhtatse tensed, probing until he felt the presence of Karenni and his small group, who were waiting in ambush in a runnel among the junipers. He felt the sharpness of their fear and excitement, smelled, even from such a distance, the stink of their sweat.

He could do nothing. He could not warn anyone, help anyone, save anyone. All that could be done by one forbidden to kill he had already accomplished. He leaned back against the gritty rock and closed his eyes, quieted his mind. And then he felt the approach of the all-devouring wind.

The first terrible gust leading the storm had not yet reached the jutting top of the mesa. It was still rolling irresistibly across the lands to the north and west, uprooting the scanty growth of brush and trees, lashing the dried grasses on the prairies, even moving stones, tumbling them along to dash them against cliffs and other rocks. This was a wind like none he had ever seen or sensed, and the force of it frightened him, bringing him upright in his niche.

His people who were on the top of the mesa would be swept away, over into the canyons. They must be warned! But how? He had no way to send a message, unless . . .

"In-teh-ka!" he called softly, cocking his head upward. "My nephew, are you there?"

The boy was supposed to be safely down in his mother's house, but Uhtatse had a feeling that he had not obeyed her commands. He had been just such a boy himself.

"Uncle?" came the small voice from above. "I am here. I could not stay with the children."

"That is well. There is a thing that you must do. Climb down to me."

There came the scrabble of hands and feet on the rock, and soon his dim shape appeared, slipping with some difficulty into the nook where Uhtatse stood. He grasped his uncle's leg to keep from falling outward and waited for orders, his face wide eyed in the growing gloom.

"Go onto the mesa, near the place where the oldest pit house was before it burned. Gather together dried juniper brush and set it alight. Take my cloak—here!" Uhtatse managed to struggle free of the garment over his shoulders and drop it into the boy's arms.

"When the fire is burning, put water from a catchment basin onto it to make it smoke. And then make puffs of smoke, using this skin. Three big heavy puffs, then two smaller ones. That is the signal that Ha-no-na-say invented, if there came any emergency while we were under attack. He will send someone to see who makes smoke and why."

"And what should I tell him?" asked the child. "What emergency is there, Uncle?"

Uhtatse pointed out and up, toward a sky that roiled with purple cloud that moved with terrible speed. Below that were layers of paler cloud, scudding even more swiftly across the troubled heavens. As the boy stared upward, his eyes widened. It was, indeed, a frightening sight.

"A wind is coming like none we have known in all our lives before," said Uhtatse. "While you tell our people, I will go and try to save our neighbors in the other clans. We must get down into the cliffs, or we will be blown away like leaves in autumn."

Again he paused and closed his eyes, feeling the currents that roiled in the sky to north and south, to east and west. "This wind comes from the north and west, rolling up the land before it. But others—devil winds—will dance out of the south and west.

"There will be no place to shelter if we are not inside the cliffs. Tell Ha-no-na-say's messenger that. Tell him that I have gone to our kinsmen, and that I will return if I can. If not, then give him my love and my farewell."

The boy gulped audibly. Uhtatse felt him holding back tears as he tied the cloak about him and moved out of the niche and again onto the cliff wall. He felt a great lump in his throat as the little shape dwindled.

"For you as well, my nephew, there is love. Remember."

In-teh-ka had reached the top. Again, his voice drifted down to his uncle. "And for you, my uncle. Farewell."

Uhtatse drew his strength together as one would a winter garment, clothing his spirit in it, sharpening his courage to go out onto the mesa, where in only a few hours that chaos of winds would devastate the land. He climbed once more, holding his feelings in check, and set out at a trot toward the nearest of the other clans of the Ahye-tum-datsehe.

Even as he ran, he felt the clash of the first group of his people with the Tsununni taking place behind him. Inside his mind he heard a tumult of shouts and the echoes of blows in the darkness.

He felt a torch being lit, and he smelled blood, even above the tang of piñon and juniper bruised by the battering they were receiving. Tsununni were coming over the edge of the cliff, and desperate figures were striking them with clubs, stabbing them with long sharpened poles, forcing the ash and mud-striped figures of the climbers back over the cliff. He could hear in his heart the cries that trailed behind some as they fell.

Now others of his groups were engaged. He felt anxiously toward those left to guard the homes in the cliff, but no enemy had been able to come at them from below. Only one had been discovered, he thought, and he felt the astonishment of the strange warrior at finding a house in such a place.

Even as he tensed, willing those inside to kill the enemy, there came a thrust from a sharpened stick. The Tsununni grunted as the point went into him, and Uhtatse felt the same stab of anguish the man felt as he was pushed away from his handholds and into space. This one would not live to tell anyone of the thing he had learned about the homes in the caves.

Uhtatse leaned with the urgency of his stride, as well as against the wind, which had now begun to wash over the mesa in long waves of violence. But his mind was back there with his people, his family.

Despite the storm, more Tsununni climbed and reached the top, and now they came up more than one route. Those stationed to repel them were attacked from behind, and with anguish and grief Uhtatse felt his kinsmen die. He could not be certain which, for in the confusion of his spirit it was only life he felt—the warm spark followed by an instant of pain and then an emptiness where that spark had burned.

The sky was black now, and the lands about were dark, with murky shapes of the scrubby trees whipping in gusts of wind that grew stronger as time passed. Grit stung his face as Uhtatse moved up and down the uneven way, his feet taking the path they knew so well, though he could not see it.

Ahead, he felt another conflict, which grew more immediate as he came nearer. Other groups of Tsununni had come from different directions, climbed the brutal walls of the mesa, and now neared more of the clans there.

They were attacking those living in the village for which he was headed, for many of those clansmen had chosen to remain in their pueblo atop the cliff. These people were without the protection of the impossible puzzles of the downward paths, and once the enemy was at hand they were far more vulnerable than his own village.

Uhtatse smelled blood, and his gut hurt with a thrust that killed someone ahead of him in the darkness. How many times must the One Who Smelled the Wind die before he was given the peace of his own death? Again he felt the instant of pain, the emptiness, and he wanted to cry out like an eagle, far above the earth, Why do men kill? Why do men kill?

Now the junipers were whipping at him as painfully as the wind, flailing into his face. He could hardly see, so filled with grit were his eyes, and his tongue tasted of blood. Ahead, his people were dying, dying, and he ran until he felt that his chest was filled with fire and his skull with pressure that threatened to burst it.

He did not slow his flying feet as he struggled to draw a deep breath and fill his lungs. "Go!" he shouted. "Go down into the cliffs! There is death coming on the wind! Let the Tsununni offer their bodies to the gods and their blood to the stone! We will die if we stay on the mesa! I, Uhtatse, warn you!"

He could sense the astonishment of those who heard that ghostly call out of the murk. But they knew that only one would come through such weather with such a word. They would talk hastily, he knew; he could hear astonished murmurs in the ears of his spirit.

He knew that some would go and some would stay, believing that this must be some ruse of the enemy. But it was the best he could manage, for there were others to warn still, and his time was becoming short.

He could still feel the deaths behind him in his own village, smell the blood that he shared with those who bled the mesa red. He could not bear to leave any he might reach to suffer the same end. Still he ran, his old heart pumping steadily, his breath coming painfully, and his legs growing more and more leaden as he moved. If the wind did not slay him, he knew the effort might, but he did not stop. He must save all of his people that he could.

He wondered suddenly if any of the other Ones Who Smelled the Wind among the people of the mesa had sensed the coming of the storm. Then he knew . . . he was the only one. No other on the mesa had the range and the sensitivity to pick up dangers so distant.

Sickness among the animals, strangers at the door they could sense, and they did that task well. But only he had shed his flesh and danced with the eagles. Only he could now warn of the violence of that storm, which might easily seem to be only one such as they had known before.

And now he began to feel the growing unease of the invading warriors. Those in the Middle Way were lashed with oak branches, the leaves so sharp with the force of the gusts that they cut like knives.

They came with dread in their blood-hungry hearts, but still they moved toward the high bastions of the mesa, and he could not help but admire their courage. Even with death bearing down upon them from the darkened sky, the Tsununni held firm to their purpose.

There could not be, among them, one such as he who could sense the weather with such accuracy. If there had been, they would have chosen another, better day for their attack. Did the gods smile on the Ahye-tum-datsehe by sending their enemies to them along with this unheard-of wind?

Again he felt movement ahead of him. The nature of those before him on the cliff was alien, the smell unlike that of his own kind, but now he knew them, for he had sensed them for most of this terrible day. Tsununni moved before him, coming up from the Middle Way along a cranny that he had used himself as a boy, exploring and hunting and making mischief.

The watchers there at its top would already have taken the word to their people, so he circled, keeping his steps light, even though the whistle of the wind was now so loud as to make them inaudible even to him. He would come to these people in time.

He ran into the Meeting Place of the last clan on his own mesa to sense a group of warriors hidden among the junipers, waiting there for their enemies to arrive. "Wind!" he gasped. "Terrible wind! Get below, my kinsmen, for as ferocious as the Tsununni may be, this storm will be worse. Let them face it alone."

He dropped to his knees, gasping for breath, and one of the young men knelt beside him. "The storm? Shall I take the word to the other mesa's clans?"

Uhtatse could only nod, for his breath was lancing through his chest in horrible stabs of pain, and his lips would no longer move. He heard the youth's steps for a moment, and then the gusts obliterated the sound, as Eeh-ya-to, the shaman of this clan, caught him up in his arms and carried him to the nearest path down into the cliffside.

Uhtatse felt himself handed down from one set of hands to the next, like a bundle of sticks or a stone for the fire pit, but he was too exhausted to object. Indeed, he was grateful that these people risked themselves to carry him to safety.

Once they gained the lip of stone that edged the cave below, the pressure of wind lessened, though it howled painfully in the crevices of the weather-worn sandstone forming their shelter. Crowding into the biggest house in the cliff, they laid him on a pile of grass-stuffed skins, and Eeh-ya-to's women gave him tiny sips of water until he could again swallow and speak.

He had arrived only a short time before the full blast of the storm. He hoped that the young man who had gone with the word to the other mesa had taken shelter, for he could not have reached his goal before the great roar in the sky became all-encompassing.

Even in the cave-house, huddled inside stone walls as he was, Uhtatse felt the pounding of the wind and the slashing rain, which penetrated even the knife-edge crannies between the stones. Yet even over the chaos of the tempest, he felt the terror of the Tsununni as they faced that devastation.

He felt enemy warriors fling themselves flat or cling to trees that were ripped from their tough old roots and whirled away into the gloom of the boiling sky. He felt their deaths, too, and they were no different from those of his own people. Was it that there was no difference between man and man, whatever his tribe or clan?

Uhtatse closed his eyes tightly, for his mind felt battered by the events of the day. He wanted to rest, to sleep, losing himself in wild dreams of riding the gentle winds of summer beside the eagles. But he could not close out the terrible things happening above him in the forest.

Through eyes not his own he saw the twisting tails of the devil winds dancing among the pueblos, cutting swaths through the junipers, laying low the piñons. He felt the despair of men caught up in irresistible and invisible hands of wind and swept away into nothingness, their spirits lost and filled with dread.

Uhtatse wanted to scream, to weep, to grieve for them, even as he did for his own.

Stop! he tried to command himself, but there was no pause in his perception as his own village, high and low, was whipped and brutalized by this storm among storms. One who could feel a leaf die when a deer nipped it from its parent tree must die many hands of times as leaves and trees and grasses, animals and men fell to the assault of the wind.

He lay there, still and silent, hoping, amid his anguish, that his own people had gained the shelter of their houses. Hoping that In-teh-ka had given the message clearly and that Ha-no-na-say's messenger had been swift.

Someone touched his hand in the darkness. "It is I, Kay-leh-tah. Welcome, brother, and our thanks for your warning. We would have been caught on the surface without it, and the wind would have swept us away into the deeps, as it has done to many of our enemies, I hope. I have not the gift to sense a storm so distant that moves so quickly. I freely admit it."

Uhtatse squeezed the callused fingers in his own. There had been, over the years, some jealousy of his reputation among the four or five Ones Who Smelled the Wind serving the clans. His idea for the cliff houses had angered some of the older ones, and its success had disturbed them even more. But now he felt that they would not resist his warnings and his advice with the determination they had shown in the past.

The noise grew terrible ... stones carried across how many spans of country rattled like weapons against the walls of the house. Thin screeches of wind penetrated the walls and made the door-skins flap desperately, tethered though they were at top and bottom and sides.

Amid the tumult, Uhtatse strained to feel what was happening to his own clan. Surely he could feel his sister, Karenni, Natosi, In-teh-ka! But no individual was distinguishable. He tried desperately to find how his own band fared.

But he could not. The uproar of the wind and grit and blowing fragments of trees and plants, the terror of the animals, small and large, as they sheltered as best they could, the pain of the junipers and piñons as they felt their branches and needles and bark stripped away by the abrasive wind all combined to blind and deafen him to those he most wanted to feel.

He lay in the strange house, clasping a stranger's hand, surrounded by grateful but unfamiliar people, and he endured. It was not the sort of thing he had dreaded before. Battle and pain were one sort of endurance. This was an entirely different kind, sent by the gods of wind and rain to aid—or to hinder?—his beleaguered kind.

Tomorrow, he hoped, he would know the answer.

△△

XLI

▽▽▽

The night was long and loud, and the house grew hot with the many bodies sheltering there, no matter that the wind whined through the smoke hole as it whipped around the doorskin to enter. Uhtatse did not sleep. He did not even rest, weary as he was, for his body was as tense as a bowstring, and his heart was filled with fear for his own.

From time to time, the people about him would shift their positions, another of their elders coming to sit beside him and touch his hand. They could talk little, so noisy was the storm, but from time to time there came a lull, and he could learn who now was nearby.

When the great wind moved onward, past the mesa, and the night grew still except for the rain, he gave a deep sigh. What had happened could not be changed, whatever it might be. But at least it was over and the damage was done. He could relax now and sleep. He turned on his side, whispered a last word to the Old Woman of this clan, who sat on the stone floor near his head, and fell into deep slumber.

The first chink of light around the door-skin woke him. The room was empty now, except for the Old Woman, who dozed against the wall, her mouth open and her hands limp in her lap. He slid past her and stepped out of the door, carefully pulling the skin shut behind him. With his heart thudding anxiously, he turned to find the way upward, down which he had come in the dark.

It was not easy to climb it. He was sore and still weary, and his legs felt as if they were wavering beneath his weight, but he persisted, feeling his way carefully. These people had also chipped out their hand- and footholds so as to confuse anyone unfamiliar with living in the cliffs, and there were places that almost puzzled him. But he gained the top at last and looked out over the mesa.

He was now almost at the northern end, and he could see for a long distance across the lower lands. The air was clear and bright, the colors hard edged, washed clean by the torrential rains. The shape of the land below was subtly different, and he knew that it was because much of the growth there was gone, leveled or carried away by the wind.

He turned, hesitant and afraid, and looked back over the rolling series of small canyons that formed the top of the mesa. His spirit

chilled, for the junipers that gave bark for
cordage, needles for tea, shade for weary people, stringers for roofs, had been twisted and
torn, some uprooted, many gone altogether.
The land about looked as if some demented
child had laid waste to it, and the catchments
that this clan was even now working to restore
had been flooded and silted in with dirt washed
from higher ground.

Their gardens, too, were flattened, the corn
so sodden with wet and mud that the stalks
were almost invisible. His own clan's food supply was in similar condition, he knew all too
well.

Kay-leh-tah came from behind him and
touched his shoulder. "Do not grieve, my
brother. If you had not come, it would be the
people who lay in ruin, not their fields. We will
survive, though the winter may be hungry. We
will go into the lower country and hunt game to
dry. We will range far and gather every grass
seed or berry that promises nourishment, as
your own clan will do. If we were dead, there
would be no hope at all." He sighed, staring off
across the crystalline distance.

"I can feel it in my heart to pity the Tsununni. They had no One Who Smells the Wind
to warn them of the storm. Those we left to
conquer our place up here on the surface are
gone as if they had never been. Not even a
feather or a weapon is left to say that they were
here."

Uhtatse nodded. "I must go now to find my clan and to see what has happened there. We had, I think, more of the enemy to deal with than did you, farther down the mesa. I find myself fearful. ... Who can know which ones among those of my family have gone into the Other Place since yesterday?

The other man raised his hand in farewell and turned back to help his people glean what they could from the ruins of their gardens. Uhtatse moved away toward his own place, staring this way and that, missing some old grandsir of a juniper from its spot or finding a veteran piñon stripped of its branches, the bare stub smelling resinous in the bright sun. All the air was sharp with the scent of broken plants.

The little canyons ran with water, the runnels having already sent their burdens of moisture into the lower ways. The air was so clean and sharp that it almost hurt his lungs as he hurried along the path, which had been washed so harshly that the pebbles sparkled clean and the grit was altogether gone.

The morning was so fine, so beautiful, that it hurt his heart to think what losses it might contain for him. As he came within sight of the Meeting Place, he saw that people were moving about, some from the direction of the gardens, some with cloths and jars in their hands, some limping.

He shouted, a long yell containing no words. A short, rugged shape appeared around the corner of the stone wall and raised a hand. Ha-no-na-say lived. That was good.

He broke into a run and came to a halt beside his old friend. "How is it with our people?" he asked. He did not say any word about his own . . . that could come when he knew that the People were in a condition to survive the winter. The clan came first. His own heart must wait its proper turn.

"The Tsununni killed many. Even though we surprised them in many places as they came over the edges of the cliff, they are fierce and terrible warriors. Natosi . . . is dead. He went over with the enemy he grappled with, hurled down into the canyon below. My heart grieves with yours, Uhtatse."

Uhtatse bent his head for a moment. Then he looked up. "Yet we prevailed? When the wind came, were we overcoming our enemies?"

"We were in place. Not a single Tsununni came into any of the cliff houses. Few penetrated as far as the gardens, and those were killed by the people hiding among the junipers and in the runnels. But we lost twelve of our people, four women, eight men. And a child was wounded . . . badly wounded. I grieve to tell you that it is your nephew In-teh-ka. He warned everyone of the storm, running from group to group, paying no heed to the fighting around him. As we drew away, disengaging from the enemy as if we were afraid, we carried him with us in the last group.

"A wounded man struck upward with his knife, and the boy was cut deeply in the hip and the leg. He lost much blood before the Healer could stop the bleeding. We are well, Uhtatse. Go to your nephew. He needs you, and he deserves to have you at his side."

"My sister?" asked the One Who Smelled the Wind. "Karenni?"

"Karenni is wounded also. Go to the House of Healing, for he is there, with your nephew. Your sister is well and is in the gardens, trying to find something more to rescue from the mud."

Uhtatse touched his old friend lightly on the shoulder. "We live, Ha-no-na-say. Whatever our losses, whatever the hardship to come, we live. Kay-leh-tah of the northern clan told me that before I left him, and I have thought of it as I came. It comforts me. Perhaps it will also comfort you."

Then he turned to run toward the House of Healing, which was located on the mesa top, near a source of water and convenient to the paths of the Healer and her helpers. His nephew had survived the night. He had known when he sent the boy to warn the others that it was a dangerous thing to do. If the child had died, he would have carried that pain, beside the others in his overburdened spirit, for as long as he lived.

The wind was whining now, though with less force by far than it had on that terrible night.

Even now, the loss of Natosi was a grief in his heart, but Uhtatse knew that before long he would join his old friend in the Other Place, and they would talk of the many things that had come to the People in the long years since that attack of the Tsununni.

It had not been the last, but years had passed before the Fierce People again turned their faces toward the mesa. That night had swept most of their warriors to their deaths, leaving the old and the women and the very young to grieve for them in the lowlands.

The bodies had been gathered up, a few at a time as the swoops of the vultures had revealed where they landed in the rough country below the cliffs. Their people had hidden themselves as best they could by day, but they had come out in the evening to take away the corpses of their fellows.

The Ahye-tum-datsehe had watched them, but they had not moved against the shattered remnant of the tribe. If they had fought bitter battles all up and down the mesa, losing too many of their own and gaining a burden of anger and grief, it might have been different. But the Wind God had raised his fist, and the Tsununni had suffered its blow.

They felt a strange sympathy for those bereaved ones who had wailed into the night their chants of grief. Uhtatse still could feel the grief he had sensed in them all the time they remained below to find their dead and release

them into the Other Place. When that was done,
they fled westward, as if the storm carried them
before it.

He shivered in the breeze. His feet were numb.
His backside hurt from the cold stone, for it had
been years since he had possessed any padding
of fat and muscle. He was ready for the thing
that came next, and yet it would not come. He
had not traveled all the way up the road of his
life. Years still divided him from that battle and
the storm.

He twisted on the boulder and pulled his
cloak closer about him. The lights had gone out
long ago there below him, and only the stars
bore him company as he relived the past.

Yet what was there of importance to remember still? The years had flowed past. In-teh-ka
had grown, though permanently crippled from
the injury to his hip. His sister had died, leaving
Karenni to grieve almost as bitterly as he had
when Ihyannah left him.

But there had been something . . . and then he
remembered the woman. Yes, that had been a
thing of importance and interest. The woman
had come from the plains . . .

XLII

It had required many days to return the life of the Ahye-tum-datsehe to something like normal. The people had feared much. They had fought hard. They had lost many of their own. Such a night as they had spent amid the winds of the world did not leave them untouched, and Uhtatse was among those most saddened.

His only real happiness came to him when he sat by the side of his nephew as the boy lay on a blanket beneath the wind-stripped juniper, watching as the others harvested grass seeds or caught chipmunks or moved away downward to hunt game in the Middle Way. And even that was becoming a difficult task, for so many clans now lived on the mesa that when all were forced to depend upon the game animals for meat it strained the resources of the deer herds.

He felt the dwindling of the animals about him, and that, too, made him despondent. He had lived for so long in close communion with the birds and the beasts, the reptiles and the insects, that he felt a kinship with them that others of his kind did not. He took every opportunity to advise his own people to go all the way down into the low country, across the ways into the forests of the eastern mountains.

"We must leave some beasts to breed so that our children will not go hungry," he told them. Ha-no-na-say agreed emphatically, but when people hunger or fear a starving winter, they do not listen deeply to the words of wise men, no matter how well meant they may be.

So he told his nephew tales of the things he had seen in his long life, stories of the visits of the Anensi, the raids of the Kiyate, almost forgotten now in the greater danger of the Tsununni. He tamed another turkey, hoping that In-teh-ka might have a feathered friend to rival the legendary To-ho-pe-pe, but others of the breed seemed less intelligent than his old friend had been.

When he was not needed to help with the injured or to keep the very young from straying while their parents worked, he ranged the height, sending his sensing far over the countryside below the mesa. He did not expect anything dangerous—it had been his experience that terrible perils came very far apart. The coming of the enemy and the storm on the same night was the first time he had known something of the sort to happen, even among the legends he had been taught as a boy.

So it was with some surprise that he found himself feeling the approach of someone who was still among the distant mountains. This was not a person running for her life ... that sort of desperation came to him clearly now. Yet she was filled with pain and anger and a terrible need.

He wondered if she would find the mesa. Indeed, he wondered if she would ever find release for her anguished fury. He could not know what had brought it about, for his gift did not extend to thoughts of people unless they were very close to him, and yet he had his own idea what might bring a person to such a pitch of intense effort.

As his nephew improved, he returned to his methodical rounds of the mesa, sensing the breath of oncoming winter, still far away in the northwest, where the storm gods lived. But even as he noted the small things that were his charge and duty, he also felt the approach of the woman across the miles. She was coming to the mesa, he was now certain, and he wondered if she might be following a trail ... a trail now cold and obscured by the storm, yet visible enough to be a guide to one with eyes sharpened by a need for vengeance.

She was, he decided, pursuing the Tsununni. Those warriors who had survived the storm, together with the families who had waited the outcome of the battle down in the lowland, had fled westward after gathering their dead following their terrible defeat. Uhtatse suspected that they feared a people who could call up the very winds to defend their homes, and he wished strongly that he could do just that at need.

When the woman came within few days' journey of the mesa, Uhtatse went down to meet her. She was in such pain that it filled his mind and body, scouring him with harsh needles of anguish. He must find what her need might be and help her to fulfill it, or else he must kill her, for her pain was now so strong that he could hear and feel nothing beyond that single outcry.

His muscles were not so flexible as they had been, his breathing not so easy. He was getting old, and the events of the past weeks had taken their toll upon his endurance, yet the One Who Smelled the Wind had never consulted his body before driving it to do his will. So he went down the steeps to the Middle Way, followed the grassy tracks of the deer even farther, and soon found himself moving across the country he had covered before.

It was clear now. She was definitely following the trail of the Tsununni, coming faster as she drew nearer the mesa. Uhtatse found himself wishing that he could float, as he had done when he went on that bodiless journey, over the rough countryside as he went to meet her, but he pushed his aching legs to a spot where he waited for her to approach him. That, he thought, would alarm her less.

She came with twilight to the place beside the stream where he had seen the camp of the enemies. She was watching the ground, stooping from time to time to pick up a lost arrowhead or a strip of rawhide or a crumple of moss that had been used to diaper a baby. The Tsununni feared no one, and they did not hide their trail. Anyone who found them was their prey, Uhtatse now understood.

When she looked up to survey the campsite further, Uhtatse smiled and held out his hands to show that he held no weapon. "Peace," he said in his own tongue, but she showed no sign of understanding.

Instead, her hand dropped to her side and came up with a flint knife. She gathered her strength for a moment and then leaped toward him, obviously intending to kill him with the last of her strength.

He stepped back and held out his hands again. In the trade language he had learned from the Anensi, he said, "Peace. The ones you hunt are gone forward, and you will not catch them now."

The words seemed to remove the last of her strength, and she dropped to her knees, the knife falling to the ground beside her. Her head bent, and she gasped, long harsh breaths seeming to carry her very spirit outward through her mouth. He knew such pain—had felt it when his son was lost and when Ihyannah leaped to her death, although he had never allowed himself the luxury of letting it out of himself.

He knelt beside her and took her thin, dirty hand into his. "Woman, be comforted. The gods of the winds themselves have scoured most of the Tsununni warriors from the world. Those who are left are the old, the very young, and the pregnant women. Come with me to our mesa, and we will give you food. If you want to go forward, then go with new strength after a rest."

Without speaking, she rose and resettled the skimpy buffalo robe pack she carried slung across her back. She stared into his eyes as he rose to face her, and he found that she was taller than he by half a hand. An unusual woman.

He nodded toward the mesa, which was hidden beyond the trees and the last of the hills. "Follow me," he said. "That is where you want to go, for there the Tsununni went. We lost many lives, even with the help of the storm, but we have our stone houses set into the cliffsides, and our families are safe." He turned and started homeward, and behind him he felt a lessening of that driving compulsion, the deafening shout of pain that had brought him across the miles.

The two camped soon, and he made fire and fed her some of the dried meat he had brought with him. That put new life into her, and they made good time over the next days.

The scent of juniper and piñon met him as they reached a spot from which they could see the high golden stone that thrust against the sky, marking the place he called home. The woman paused, awed and startled at that tremendous cliff, which even the remaining distance could not dwarf. She stared at him questioningly, but he shook his head.

"We will talk later," he said, finding it hard to say what he wanted in the trade language. "There is one there who can speak better."

So they went onward, and when they began to climb past the Middle Way, she kept up with him effortlessly. He saw now that she was a young woman still, though worn and haggard with grief and effort.

The watcher replied to his signal as he started up the difficult way to the top of the mesa, and when the two of them reached the top there were several warriors there. The attack had made his people cautious, and all of the clans kept armed men alert for anything unusual. But all of them knew Uhtatse, and he nodded as they raised hands in greeting, passing through the small group toward the end of the mesa on which his own people lived.

"What are you called?" the woman asked in halting trade language. She had not spoken before, and he accepted her words as a good omen.

"I am Uhtatse, the One Who Smells the

Wind. My people are the Ahye-tum-datsehe. We have lived here since the sun kindled its fires, the moon first shone silver on the land . . ." but he realized that he had lapsed into his own tongue, and he smiled apologetically, gesturing toward his home.

Ra-onto would talk with this woman and find what tragedy had sent her wandering over the land, filled with loss and fury.

XLIII

And so it was. The old man on the cliff, with his infallible memory, still could live every moment of the story that had emerged as the woman, Seeing Bird, talked with Ra-onto, partially in trade language, partly in her own barbaric tongue, which the Anensi understood a bit, and partly through sign language.

Even now, sitting at the edge of the cliff, surrounded by his own death, he remembered the pain he had felt as the story unfolded.

XLIV

The breeze came steadily from the west for three days after the attack on the hunting camp. On the third day, Seeing Bird was given a vision. Her son was alive, a captive, being borne away into that dry wind by those who had taken him after killing his father and his uncle.

Once she was certain, she said nothing, even to her grieving mother. She slung a buffalo robe pack over her shoulder, tucked into it an extra pair of moccasins, and hung her grandmother's flint knife from her belt-rope. She would find her son, or she would kill those who destroyed him if he died in days to come.

Behind her, the village was silent, though she knew that many watched her go. They, too, had their losses and their griefs, but only she had been given a dream to guide her. She did not look back.

She was too thin for such a demanding journey, but the fasting in preparation for the dream had taken flesh from her bones. Yet there was no time to build her strength again. The Tsununni had taken her son, and every hour meant that they had traveled farther along their path. If she was to catch up with them, she must go at once.

The breeze was fitful on her face, sometimes dying away but always returning and always from the west. It was a sign, she knew, and she walked steadily, hour after hour.

The sun crossed the sky above her and moved down to shine directly into her face. Her moccasins moved quietly over the grass, but she didn't look down. Her gaze was set on the horizon, as if by the strength of her vision she might hinder the travel of the Tsununni. The sun sank, and the sky turned lilac and orange and a clear, strange shade of green, but she did not slow her gait until darkness came down across the flat country and hid the ground from her eyes.

Only when she stumbled to her knees and could no longer rise did she unroll her robe and take from its depths a bit of jerky and the gourdful of water she had brought. She allowed herself two sips of the water, for she was now in a country that held little in summer. She chewed the tough meat, morsel by morsel, making a small piece last for a long while. When she lay back on the robe, even the howling of coyotes at the half moon could not prevent sleep from coming.

Even then, she did not rest well, dreaming always that she was running forward toward the vision of her son, who receded before her, always unreachable, always calling for her. A child of three summers was so easily killed!

She woke before moonset. There was a milky circle of mist around the moon. There would be rain or storm in time. She had been bred in flat country that bred tornados, and she was no stranger to their destructive power.

She set out again, her feet crushing the tall grass that swished about her waist as she assessed the general direction of her quarry and cut across untracked spaces in order to save time. They were headed north and west, and she cut their track often enough to be certain that she was correct.

The remnant of her vision still clung about her. She felt that she weighed nothing, her feet falling as gently as leaves against the ground, her pack insubstantial against her back. The distance she had come was unimportant, and that to travel still was not considered. She would go as far as need be. When she found her son, she would stop.

She kept her thoughts from straying to Sun-Hawk, her husband. He was dead, and she could not help him. Their son was still alive. Deer-Child was ahead of her, and she would move toward him as long as her body held life.

She found his corpse at the first camp the Tsununni made in the mountains. They had not troubled themselves to wrap it and put it into a tree, and wild animals had torn it. But she knew her son, even if he had no face left for her to see.

She knew there had been no chant sung over him, to give a good journey into the Other Place. Those things she did herself, coldly, feeling strangely removed from her actions.

She used half her robe to wrap him, binding the hide tightly with strips of bark. She climbed high into a squat prairie tree and tied the small body firmly into a crotch. Then she sang a death song for him, who had been too young to sing his own. No tear touched her eyes, and she did not rend her clothing or tear her hair, as was proper in normal circumstances. She was controlled as she left him to his long rest and took up the journey again.

Before, she had drifted like a leaf in the wind, pulled effortlessly by the life of her son before her. Now she was propelled like an arrow from a bow, a weapon aimed at the hearts of her enemies. She went even faster as the flesh melted away from her bones, her heart burned more and more hotly in her chest, and the lives of the Tsununni called to her to spill them onto the ground.

It was that burning need that drove her to the spot where Uhtatse met her. He often won-

dered how quickly she had covered those long
distances over which the Tsununni had traveled lazily, using up their last loot before reaching the place where they intended to replenish
their supplies.

Once she had rested and eaten well, she came
back slowly into herself as a living being. She
had, he thought, been more spirit than flesh as
she raced over prairie and mountains toward
her goal. Once she lost the compulsion of the
dream, she seemed lost and very lonely.

He had known the pain she suffered, for the
edge of his own losses had never dulled with
time. She was lonely and so was he, so they
comforted each other over the following winter.
When she died, still thin and sick from her journey, spring was new, and he had another loss to
set beside his older ones. He found himself hoping that she had discovered, in the Other Place,
her son with Ihyannah and his own child.

*The ancient man found that he had been sit-
ting with his eyes closed. His legs were numb
with cold, and he could no longer feel his fingers. The wind blustered about him, flapping
the fringes of his robe with soft flutterings
against the rock on which he sat.*

*Had the time come? Only years of work and
growing weariness followed Seeing Bird's death
and that of his sister. The attacks of the Tsununni, after that major one, were relatively mi-*

nor, for the Ahye-tum-datsehe now knew how to deal with them.

The houses in the cliffsides grew more numerous, until everyone lived in safety below, except in the summer, when they camped in the old pueblos in order to tend the crops and drive away the deer that foraged in the plantings. The decision to build in the cliffs had, Uhtatse knew, saved his people . . . perhaps from complete annihilation. That was a joy to him, and few men he had ever known could credit themselves with such an important idea.

He put his hands on the stone and heaved upward, his bones creaking with pain and cold. Now it was time. His work was done, and there was no one to grieve at his going.

He made his way along the edge of the cliff, toward the spot from which Ihyannah had dived. Much of it had crumbled away into the deep, over the years, but there was still a ledge of rock onto which he lowered himself, careless now whether he made it or not.

When he stood there, the wind was shut away by the cliff behind him, and the gulf below was deep in darkness. No twinkle of light from the caves on the other side of the canyon bade him farewell as he stepped forward, singing, and went to find his death.

AFTERWORD

In 1970, the mummies of a small boy and an old man were housed in the museum atop Mesa Verde. The child had been found in a crevice, down which he had evidently fallen, and he looked so alive that an observer felt that he might open his eyes and speak. The old man had been buried at the back of one of the caves, behind the house.

On a return trip, in 1984, I found both bodies gone, and those in attendance at the museum at that time knew nothing of them. However, in the interim, sometime during the seventies, I had seen a newspaper item that mentioned that two mummies had been stolen from the Mesa Verde museum. I hope that they were taken by their own kind of people, distant kin though they might be, and put to rest, at long last, with all the proper rituals.